From Fear to Freedom

Eagle Annie

Balboa Press books may be ordered through booksellers or by contacting:

Balboa Press
A Division of Hay House
1663 Liberty Drive
Bloomington, IN 47403
www.balboapress.com.au
1 (877) 407-4847

Print information available on the last page.

ISBN: 978-1-4525-2761-1 (sc)
ISBN: 978-1-4525-2762-8 (e)

Balboa Press rev. date: 02/10/2015

Sarshas Roses

Sasha did not know how long she had been there, nor why she even went there, or where she had been before she went there. All she did know for sure was that she could hardly breathe any more. The air was thick and musty, smelling strongly of decaying flesh. She was now quite desperate to get away from there.

It was so dark she could hardly recall anything being as dark as that before. Sasha ached to be out of that darkness where she actually felt as though she was dying.

That was it; she had finally had enough so made up her mind that now was the time to make a move for freedom and if necessary at any cost. She had determined to leave and never return. After all who would want to go back to such a frightening place?

Slowly she became aware that her thoughts were becoming much more defined, then she also realised it had been a very long time since she had been able to think in that way.

It frightened her to see that her thoughts had suddenly become clear and decisive, for she now knew she alone had to face up to them and deal with them for herself.

She became tired and struggled with the awareness of her responsibility. Again her thoughts began to run riot as they started to scream, this is not fair, this is not fair in any way, why am I even in this place, somehow I must find out.

Sarsha then knew it would be vitally important to know the reason why she was there so she could avoid returning there at any later time.

Her instincts kept telling her over and over, Find out the reason, find out the reason, or you will end up here again, but next time you may not be able to leave.

At this point she realised she could hear a small, gentle voice calling out to her above the sound of her own racing thoughts. It was different to any other she had previously heard and it was causing her to move towards the sound of those foreign yet, clearly spoken words.

She quickly spun around to attempt to find out where it was coming from. As she turned she almost fell over something. With fear and trembling she realised that someone or something else was in that place besides her. No other sound was heard, just the sense that something was so close that her skin prickled as the invisible whatever, slowly moved nearby. She began to panic and started to grope her way around what seemed to be a rock wall and headed towards the sound of that voice which was still tenderly calling out to her.

Bit by bit she carefully edged forwards, stumbling many times. Again her fear intensified as she began to realise that what previously seemed to be solid walls were in fact constantly moving and changing places.

Nothing was staying the same; nothing was familiar to her any more.

By now she was so totally gripped with fear that it made the small voice seem to move so far away that she could hardly hear it.

Sarsha thought that there now seemed to be another factor about that strange voice which she had not recognised before. It was constantly steady with a warm, safe, comforting sound. It began to sound like a familiar tune she had heard somewhere a long time ago.

Finally after many attempts to escape that place, she fell over with exhaustion and was instantly sick everywhere. There was something so foul in there which stuck to her each time she fell, it was constantly distracting her ability to think clearly and move forwards.

Repeatedly she stood up and tried to shake off the foul smelling stuff which clung to her, during which time the small voice continued calling to her. Now the voice was becoming louder and clearer.

Again she spun around and this time she noticed a small light near what appeared to be a door way.

Now she could move forward with a strange assurance of being able to put her feet clearly on the ground and see where she was going.

I don't know where this light is coming from she thought, but I can see where my feet are going now. I know I shall find out what that light is about and where it is coming from.

At that point, she realised that the sweet, gentle voice was actually calling her by name. She was beginning to breathe the fresh air that was coming from the same direction as the light.

Sarsha, Sarsha, where have you been for so long?

I do not know she sobbed deeply, then broke down and cried as if her heart was physically breaking apart.

After that she fell asleep on the ground near the stranger's feet for many days. When she awoke, the stranger was still quietly standing there in the same position, with a warm smile on his face.

He held some strange stones in his hands.

Sarshas heart started to beat a little faster as she realised that the light coming from those stones was the same light she saw as she began to find her way out of the dark cave.

Her curiosity rose higher and higher and she began timidly to edge her way closer towards the stranger with the hope to see what he was holding that was giving off such a strange light.

As she did, she passed fully through the entrance of that dark hole which she had just left and shuddered.

But the smell of the small white flowers that were growing over the mouth of the hole quickly drew her attention. She began to look more closely at what was all around her and take notice of its beauty.

The stranger stood silently by and allowed her to take her time to investigate for herself, what was really there.

As Sarsha looked a little further down that strange pathway that lead off into an unknown distance, she saw to her great surprise, some kind of roses that were growing directly out of the ground. But strangely there wasn't any form of bush or plant to support them.

She slowly moved towards them. Then she realised, the stranger was still there right beside her and he was still holding those strange but beautiful stones in his hands.

The Frozen Tears

They were sparkling in the beauty of the early morning sunrise and had light emanating from them which delighted her and filled her with great surprise.

Sarsha, I know you are curious about these stones. Come and I shall explain what they are.

She crossed over the front of that dark smelly hole yet again and sat on the ground near the stranger's feet.

By now the stranger had sat on a rock near the front of the cave just a little off to the side.

What are they she exclaimed with excitement, even though much fear was still squeezing at the walls of her heart causing difficulty with her breathing?

Quietly the stranger began to explain to her; These he said, are all those tears you cried as you first began to enter that cave right there.

Sarsha turned and looked. Then for the first time, she realised it was a large cave, almost completely covered over by all those beautiful flowers around it. The entrance could not be clearly seen and she noticed that just behind the sweet flowers there were thorns as long as her arms.

On many of them there were pieces of dead flesh and she realised that it was the same stench as that of the things which she stumbled over inside the cave.

She was now unable to utter the words that were still trying to form themselves into real questions which she was aching to ask the stranger.

These he said again, are your tears. She looked even closer now. But they are solid and so clear and beautiful she cried. Oh yes, was his reply. I have watched you the whole way as you came from the village and were calling to you the whole time, but you could not hear me. Since that time, I have constantly stood here while you were in the cave, and have carefully collected all of your tears and kept them.

Oh dear, you are certainly a strange person, why on earth would a stranger want to collect something that has come from such a painful time of another's life she cried?

You have been in there for so long that they have turned solid out here in the cold. I have had them for many seasons and I shall keep them always for they are of great value to me and priceless beyond all measure. I shall be gathering all of these tears eventually and will be keeping them in a beautiful, large bottle in a safe place.

But what is that all around your feet she asked? They seem to be the same as those you are holding.

They are the tears of all those who are still in the cave now. She suddenly stopped talking and was almost sick again, because she instantly knew that there were other people still in there, even though she did not want to think about all that anymore.

The stranger steadily continued talking; I have picked these up to show you that they are being taken good care of.

What will you do with all those others there at your feet she asked?

They too will be picked up and shown to those who have cried them as they leave the cave.

Come with me he beckoned to her. Let us go to the village and I shall show you something, which for now you alone can do.

Again she noticed the roses on the ground and that they were pure white. She began to question him about them and many other things as she relaxed more and her sense of safety grew along with her confidence towards the stranger. Well he said, these roses are the precious and beautiful things that all those people in the cave left behind as they travelled towards the dark hole.

Still puzzled a little she decided to ask more and more of him.

What then are those things which seem to be pearls in the middle of them? And how come the flowers are still alive even though they are not growing on bushes or anything like that? How come that they are even there at all? He waited patiently till Sarsha had exhausted her efforts of asking so many questions of what this is and what that is.

Sarsha, the people only dropped them there because they no longer believed that they had the strength to carry such beautiful things any more. I saw them from the first moment they were dropped there and have been watching over them every moment since.

The things which seem to you to be like pearls are a special portion of soil that I have placed in each of them, to assist their growth, until their owners themselves are able to pick them up again and enjoy them.

What has kept them alive, she cried? Every time another child came along this road towards that cave he said, the many tears that they cried fell on the flowers and placed just enough moisture on them to keep them alive.

That same thing also happened at the same time when the adults gave up hope and dropped the precious treasures that were beautiful to them. As the children followed behind crying their little eyes out while attempting to hold on to their mummy or daddy, their tears dropped on to the flowers keeping them alive.

Within a short time, Sarsha and the stranger had reached the outskirts of the small village. Both of them were exhausted, so they sat quietly for a short while on a large tree which had fallen across the road during the last storm.

Sarsha began to recall how the stranger had said "I will show you something you can do" She now openly and frequently questioned him about that too. He explained with that same gentle, patient voice which he had used at the mouth of the cave. Even though there is no one that you know in this village, there are many of their children that have also disappeared into that cave. And because you are the first one to come out of it, you know the way back there. Only you can talk to them in a way they understand and help them decide if they want to come out or not.

The people of the village do not know where the cave is and they certainly don't know how to get into it, because the smell of the beautiful flowers would stop them from going any further and they would have no idea that there was anything unlovely behind such a sweet facade. Even if they did know something or someone was behind such a beautiful sight, they would not be able to get past the large thorns, because their fear of being torn to pieces by them would immobilize them.

Now Sarsha became really angry and cried like never before. Why should I go back to that cave for anybody, let alone for people who don't even know or like me? And definitely not for people whom I believe wouldn't bother attempting to go beyond those thorns? Why me? Why me? She angrily spat at the stranger.

Silently the stranger stood up and slowly continued on to the village. Sarsha had followed but didn't know why. As they approached a small cottage at the edge of the village they both smelt the teasing odours of good food cooking somewhere close by.

Sarsha wanted to stop and clean the smelly, sticky things off her from when she fell over in the cave. I cannot go into that cottage looking like this she moaned. She began to back away but the stranger gently encouraged her to keep going forward.

Wait a little longer Sarsha, there is a woman in there who will be happy to help you clean up and find a nice new dress for you to wear and keep.

Hesitantly she edged forwards again. But what are these sticky things she cried? They are the clothes which the people in the cave tried to put on themselves, believing it would help the thorn scratches to get better.

They could not see and did not know what they were doing, nor did they know that the clothes they tried to use were actually covered in poison and used to tie up some of the children by many nasty adults as they imprisoned them in the cave.

Sarsha reluctantly allowed the lady in the cottage to help her clean up and put on the new dress which seemed to glow in the sunlight. She then slept for the rest of the afternoon, right up till the time the stranger and the lady of the cottage were about to sit down to the evening meal.

She awoke suddenly with a fright. She could hear what seemed to be like a thunderstorm at the window. When she looked out, there were more people than she could count. All of them were calling out from a broken and anger filled heart to the stranger inside to come and help.

We have waited long enough, cant you now please tell us where all of our children are? We don't have any idea where they have gone yet we have still tried many, many times over the years to find them. We have no strength, no money and no longer any ideas as to where we should continue looking. Just exactly what are we supposed to do about them?

The stranger quietly came and stood beside Sarsha as his words came again like smooth music to her ears. This is what I was telling you that you could do he whispered.

However you need to think of this though; you alone can decide to go or not to go and help. These people do not know you and they will not be able to help for a long time yet.In fact, they may think you are strange or even wrong in the way you do things, but I will be there to help you. Now Sarsha began to suspect he was capable of doing a lot more than he had yet spoken of.

Sarsha was not in the least interested in money or any form of payment. Still she felt she had to have something, at least some good reason to go back to such a bad place, just to encourage people to come out. What if none of them would listen to her? What if they beat her up because they were still too afraid to listen to anything new or different to what they had come to know in that cold and dark place for so long? The stranger knew exactly what was racing through her fear filled mind. I will show you how to gather these stones, and he gently showed her the ones which he still had in his hands from when he was standing at the mouth of the cave. I can also show you how to put that soil which is like pearls, into the middle of those special roses. But Sarsha, you need to know, that is all I would be doing for you.

I would only teach you how to do what I have been doing, and then I will be leaving the choice up to you to carry out the actions of it or not. He then left Sarsha alone in the room to think for a while.

She went to the window again and had another look. Many of the people had become tired and had gone home, thinking the stranger was not interested enough to help them.

There was a woman who stood out amongst the rest because of her age and the apparent ugliness of her face. She just lay there on the ground as if dead. She is nothing more than an ugly old witch thought Sarsha. But still she felt compelled to ask her, woman, why aren't you going home like all the others? You too must be tired by now, after all this time of trying to get to talk to the stranger. I am indeed said the old hag, but I have had nothing to eat for so long that I can no longer move. I no longer have the strength to take care of myself, not even to cook if I had the food, not to wash myself. I can no longer think clearly and quite honestly I can't be bothered to try, I just don't care anymore. I no longer want to feel this pain let alone deal with it. I feel there is nothing left to live for since my children have gone away.

Reluctantly Sarsha began to allow a deeply rooted compassion to stir again within her. A compassion which she thought was lost and something which she wanted to stay lost. She never wanted again to feel so deeply when she could not protect many of those she had previously seen in extreme danger.

However she could not ignore the tugging of concern towards the old hag. She quietly asked her, will you give it one more try if the stranger will listen to you?

Yes said the woman, but after tonight I will not wait or try any longer.

Sarsha then turned to leave the room and go look for the stranger. He was standing in the door way right behind her. Are you ready to talk yet he asked? This time his voice was still warm and gentle, but now it carried a sense of greater strength which challenged Sarsha.

Yes, I am but I have to admit I am still a little fearful of all the possibilities of things going quite wrong, after all I am still only a young person myself. I told you before that I will be with you, was his simple response.

They had not talked for long and Sarsha already knew that she would at least be attempting to get some of those children in the cave to listen.

Her mind was so filled with thoughts of what may happen the next day that it made her forgot she hadn't eaten. She went to bed and slept again but this time more peacefully than she had for a long time.

When she awoke early the next morning there was a blanket of frost covering everything outside. Of course she wanted to stay tucked under the blankets in bed a bit longer. Come said the stranger, let us eat and drink something hot. Our first trip back to the cave will begin this morning. After the meal that was eaten in complete silence, Sarsha and the stranger quickly and quietly began to walk back to the cave. Will I have much help going back into this cave and do I have to go in there many times she asked him? I will be with you every step of the way and yes you will have to go in there more times than you can bear to think about at this time.

When Sarsha and the stranger reached the mouth of the cave, the stench of it came rushing out towards them and the thorns seemed to be sharper and uglier than she remembered. Finally she began her first trip back into the cave, although, barely just insider it.

The awareness of her promise to go back in there to encourage others to come out held her firm to the task. At the same time however there was the now constant movement among what had previously seemed to be solid walls. Each step she took caused her to stumble because of the constant, unseen but physically felt movement. She remembered well the cold fingers of fear that had clawed at her heart and immobilised her till the warm, soft voice of the stranger had persisted long enough to encourage her to come out.

As she continued to call, come on you can come out of here. I will help you. Come on, it is safe; we can go out into the light and warmth of the sunshine outside. Come on we can get something warm to eat, and have a warm bath in fresh clean water. I feel that there are many of you in there and you don't have to be afraid. I have been in here for a long time too. I know it is safe to go outside and look at all the beautiful things of nature. There are many people worried about where you are. There are many mums and dads waiting to see if their children are safe, or even alive. The more she spoke the more she heard those ever increasing, distinct noises like puppy's whimpering.

When she first arrived at the cave entrance Sarsha noticed there was just a little light in the beginning of the cave mouth, so she entered as far as she could see from it.

By that evening, after all her efforts, just one small boy had come out with her to the fresh air and sunlight. The stranger, Sarsha and the little boy went back to the village and reached the cottage just in time for the evening meal. After washing the little boy, Sarsha nursed him all evening. Much later that night, she heard what sounded like a growling dog which intermittently whimpered or howled as if it was caught in a rabbit trap. Though by now she was so tired she could hardly move, she stirred herself carefully so as not to awaken the boy which she still held closely. She went to the window to see what was making such incredible noises. What is it asked Sarsha annoyed and deeply bothered by the ugliness of the old hag which she saw again crouching on the ground?

The old woman spoke now with anger as she spat the words out. The stranger has still not spoken to me yet, so I am not coming back here again. As the old woman spoke she lifted her face to see who the voice belonged to that had now spoken to her two nights in a row.

Sarsha had moved the curtain aside slightly to see the woman on the ground more clearly. As she did this the bright moon light shone upon the little boys face. The old woman looked closer now then started screaming, my boy, my boy my boy where have you been? The noise had awoken the boy and he began to cry with fear not understanding what had made it. Mama, mama he cried out as he recognised her.

Without speaking, Sarsha gently handed the small boy to his mother and he instantly snuggled into the warmth and safety of her arms.

Sarsha was shocked to notice the sudden changes that came over the old hags face. Bit by bit it began to soften as the natural colours came back into it. The deep lines which had come over the years of heartache and sorrow began to fill out and her face actually began to shine. Even her eyes now had a gentle sparkle to them. Sarsha had never imagined anything so dramatic could possibly happen just because one small, lost child was returned to his mother's arms. Sarsha then felt that the mother was so beautiful and seriously doubted that she was anywhere near the age she originally had thought her to be. Now she deeply regretted her harsh thoughts about her.

The stranger re-entered the room enquiring as to what the fuss and noise was all about. Look said Sarsha, look, this is the first child to come out of the cave, and see, and it is the son of this old lady who has lost many children. The mother did not understand what was happening, but looked at the stranger and quietly wept. Somehow she knew that he had something to-do with her son being back in her arms again.

As she turned to go away, she looked directly at the stranger and softly whispered; thank you.

Now Sarsha, said the stranger, you can begin to gather up for me all those tears that you have seen the mother and her son cry. Without hesitation Sarsha began to do just that. As she did so, she was amazed at how beautiful, sparkling and colourful they all were. She could not understand the incredible joy which was welling up from deep inside her. But she did know that early next morning and for many days to come, she would be going backwards and forwards to that cave to give her best efforts at encouraging others to come out into the light and warmth of the day.

Will they all come out she asked the stranger? No, some have been in there for so long that they no longer believe they are able to do anything different, even though they don't like where they are.

You will have to be brave and courageous Sarsha, and do only what I show you each time you go to the cave, or the heart ache which you have known well for many years will return. You will need to accept the fact that you cannot save all of them. Not all of the lost in there want to be saved or do what I can show them in real freedom.

Just do your best and learn to move on when each part of your work has finished.

For a long time Sarsha had listened to the heartache of the parents who had lost their children. Many had done everything they knew how to find them. However, some simply became despondent and gave up trying.

But no one ever wanted to go anywhere near the actual cave to call out to their children which puzzled her continuously. Sarsha found that hard to understand in any way but constantly remembered the words of the stranger, Do only what I show you to and remember that not all are going to be brought out into the light. Sarsha also found it hard to remain patient with the parents when they refused to try to act or even speak positively about the possibilities of the freedom of the other children still left in the cave. Many children were brought out of that horrible place, till the day Sarsha went there for one last try to see if anyone else would come out. She tried for hours calling, come on come out into the light. No sound was heard all day, she no longer felt or sensed any movement within the cave where she still only stood just inside the entrance. Sadly she recognised although her was heart filled with grief that it was now time to go back to the village.

As she left the cave the stranger smiled at her and it melted more of the fear and coldness that had been within her.

Now Sarsha, it is time to go on to the next place of work which I have planned out for you.

Sarsha by then had enough peace to know she could move forwards to something new. Some residing sadness caused her to hesitate only for a few moments as the stranger came close to her and took her hands gently in his and simply looked her in the eyes and said; You have done well. You have given all that you have for this area of work and pain. Now it is time for others to take up the same work, to finish the job as they teach and train the lost children which have come out of that cave of horror. They will need to be taught all over again how to be free and live well in strength, joy, peace and the full light of the day despite what they have been through. Those things cannot be automatically done, they are to be taught.

Sarsha went back one more time to the village to say good bye to those she had come to know quite well over the period of time she had been there. She did so because of the memories which lingered strongly in her mind of situations they had been through together. She knew well many of their struggles. She had come to deeply appreciate the victory they had taken together, back from the damaging effects done unto them by others which had originally driven some of them to that ugly cave.

She knew they would have to learn a whole new way of life and that at times it would still be a real battle but that it would be well worth while the effort in the long term.

The Village Weaver

She then left the village that same day and began to travel through many towns, cities and villages, and on the odd occasion through some parts of the nearby dessert. The whole time she was travelling throughout the vast countryside, she learnt many things she would never have been able to if she had stagnated permanently in that one small place not far from the cave.

In one of the large cities she met and married a man of another culture.

They had four children. There were three girls and a boy. Soon afterwards they all moved back to the country and lived and worked on the land and in small country towns.

Within a few years the husband had died, three of the children grew up and went off to other cities and villages to live and work and start their own way of life as they attempted to make their own fortune, and one died at a very early age.

The son had gone to war for his country and came back as a totally changed person, outwardly at least. He felt like a stranger amongst his own. Not even Sarsha could reach through to his heart, to comfort and encourage or help him in any way. In the many days and indeed years of trying to reach him she was comforted as she remembered the words of the stranger, I will be with you and show you what to do.

The eldest of the children was sick from the day it was born.

Sarsha never really got to know her and the child became as a stranger to her.It was as if the child had entered another kind of a cave which Sarsha could not even enter let alone bring someone out of.

This was one of those times she knew she was unable to do anything about that child or its freedom and joy of living. In many ways she knew she had to move on and leave the work of the child's freedom for the stranger to take care of, as he showed others how to move in and do the necessary work and teaching of her.

In the hidden depths of her heart, she felt as though all her children had become as strangers to her. The younger folk seemed to live a much faster pace of life. Many of the things which were of a greater value to her personally were now left by the wayside as they discovered different and more pleasing ways to live and enjoy life. Yet she knew her work in that area of the country had to be left behind as she continued to go to all the other new places and do all the new things, that the stranger would be showing her.

She eventually came to a tiny village and settled in the cottage which was on a farm right on the border of another town. The owners had asked her to stay there and look after the place for they would not be there most of the time. It was a palace with a stream running through the centre of it where many fish were caught. There was a bounty of other wild life which were easily caught and used for food. Wood for the fire was abundant and easily gathered also. Sarsha was happy to settle here in a small cottage on the property forever and just cut off from the rest of the world. But the niggling thoughts that she may be uprooted again never quite left her. She relished the comfortable changes she experienced which each season, were brought about for her good each year.

One day in the middle of winter, as she sat alone near the wood fire, wondering what was next on the list. She sat there a long time just gazing into the mesmerising flames as they danced up and down throwing their reflections on the nearby walls. She wondered what it would be like just to go out into the bush and live alone for the rest of her days.

A sharp knock rattled her door. She rose to see who it was, a little annoyed at the interruption to her time of warmth, comfort and drifting with the images of the flames.

There stood a tall stranger with broad shoulders and a kindly face, smiling as he began to speak.

After asking her name and for some kind of identification, he then asked if she had a cup of water. He had travelled a long way which had taken many years to reach her, and now he was thirsty and hungry.

Sarsha realised she had been staring at the stranger with her mouth wide open. She apologised and stepped aside asking him to enter.

The stranger moved to the fire place warming his hands and placing his brief case on the floor nearby.

Sarsha had made some soup earlier that day and it was still simmering on the ledge near the fire. She offered the stranger some soup and a goblet of mulled wine.

He sat silently for a long time, and they both just watched the flames as they continued to dance.

Eventually Sarsha could stand the suspense no longer. So she quietly asked him why he was there, and indeed who was he.

He did not mention his name which bothered Sarsha, but not enough to deter her from listening to his reason as to why he was there.

I have some documents here Sarsha which belong to you alone.

You have grandparents who have always belonged to an ancient, royal family. All of them are now dead, and I know all your nearby relatives except your children are also dead. There is no longer any one who is entitled to do and be what these documents have laid out for you.

To receive the ongoing inheritance enclosed in these papers you must go there and live in the family palace as you take care of it.

For now that responsibility is yours alone. You shall have to become acquainted with the people of the village which surrounds the palace and learn how to care for them. Such care and support has been absent since your grandparents have died.

There is an inherited allowance which comes with this responsibility. It has already been placed in the care of the money steward in the village. No one else but you will ever have access to that money. You only have to take this document to him and he will release all that you need, as each new need arises. How shall I get there she questioned? And what is the name of the village? Come out here and I shall show you said the stranger. At the doorway stood the most powerful horse she had ever seen. Over her many years of travel she knew what it was like to live and work on many different kinds of farms. Though she had spent some of her working years in cities and towns, most of her life was living and working on the land. She remembered well the times when she had to walk several kilometres just to get to a town, village or trading post for her needs as a young adult and for her family's needs in the preceding years. This horse then, was at least a luxury to go wherever it was she was supposed to go.

With no other form of transport available to Sarsha, she knew this was her only mode of travel. What is the direction of this new village and what is its name she enquired?

First of all Sarsha, you need to put the fire out which burns in the fire place, pack just one small bag of clothing then I will show you.

Sarsha entered her tiny home again and did as the stranger had directed. Sad at leaving the place she had come to love, yet she knew she would never be back there again. The stranger helped her on to the horse and led here down to the gate way of the large property. As he let go of the bridle he pointed off to the left and said; there is the direction of your new village.

Don't allow anyone to cause you to travel in any other direction or you will miss the right place.

You need to know beforehand that during the time of your new journey you will be going through many dry places which include some hot deserts. You will have to travel over many rough tracks through wild bush land and forests. You will be climbing many hills that have some sharp and many slippery rocks. You will have to cross many high and dangerous mountains. Sarsha, after you have been travelling for a long time and have learnt many new things and suffered greatly and known much joy, much new joy, there will also come a time when you will have to dive into the very depths of the deepest and strange ocean to bring something of great value out of it. That special treasure is yours and you will need to pick it up for yourself. It is in a very dangerous part of the ocean needing great care for you to be able to gather it. No one else can collect it for themselves of for you, they do not have the ability and it does not belong to them in any form. You will know when you are ready, then you will take the appropriate journey to that specific place in the bottom of the ocean, with care and safety and gather what lays there specifically just for you.

But surely if someone wanted to help me gather some rare treasure I should honour their loving effort and allow them to do so. No Sarsha not really in this particular situation. The main reason no one else can gather the treasure for you is because even with detailed directions, they would not be able to find it. If by some accident they found the general area in the ocean they certainly would not recognise the actual treasure nor would they be able to lift it out of the depths and nor would they know how to fully look after it even for a short time. You alone are the only one being trained and prepared to do such a job with that particular treasure. Only you have the ability to appreciate the beauty and value of it. The others that would offer to gather it for you are meanwhile being trained to gather their own specific treasures that you could not recognise and from places where you could not go. Where your treasure is Sarsha it lays in a dangerous place for anyone who is not trained and prepared to go to. So for now you just keep on going as you follow these same kinds of markings on this small map and learn all that you can in each place you go to and from each person that you meet. The name of the village where I am sending you is called Malkendah.

He then handed her a map which had been printed on very old parchment. There were distinct markings which she now recognised in the layout of the land near her own home, but never knew what they were or why they were there. There were many strange rocks in regimented order with unusual patterns and markings near her which now seemed to come alive.

She turned to say good bye to the stranger but he was gone. Only then did she realise that he was familiar somehow and had some of the same ways as the stranger she met at the door way of the cave so many years earlier.

Momentarily she hesitated, should she go and stir up the old fire and sit with its comfort and warmth just a little longer?

From the difficulty she had in mounting the horse with the strangers help, she instantly knew it was going to be even more difficult to dismount without his help later. By now she felt compelled to go on that unknown journey, so she gently nudged the horses flank and they set off. By night fall she knew they had travelled a greater distance than she previously thought possible. When the darkness of night had encompassed them, without thinking about it, Sarsha dismounted and tied the horse to a fallen tree amongst the trees at the edge of the forest she had come to.

She realised the flavour of the hot soup which she had shared with the stranger at lunch time still remained in her mouth and hunger didn't become a necessary thing she had to pay attention to at that time. As she went to look for some blankets on the back of her horse to make up a bed in the ferns nearby, she remembered that she had only packed a small bag as directed by the stranger. An unusual peace filled her heart and she lay down near the horse and allowed the warmth of the forest to cover her. It was only a short time before she was in a deep sleep.

Early the next morning as the fog began to swirl throughout the forest; she could smell the distinct and beautiful perfume of a wood fire close by.

As she stirred she could hear the horse stirring also and wondered why it seemed so close. She turned her head and saw that it had lay down beside her and remained there the whole night.

She rose then to investigate where the fire was coming from and to prepare for the next part of her journey. As she stood to full height, she saw just the other side of the fallen tree a small camp fire with a tin billy hanging on a stick above it. There on a tin plate sitting on some smaller rocks was a plate filled with cooked fish. A hand written note with beautiful script read; Sarsha I trust you will enjoy this meal I have left for you. The tea is nice hot but can be drunk cold as well. Horse began to graze close by as Sarsha sat on the fallen tree and thoroughly enjoyed the meal of fish and unusually sweet tasting tea.

When she finished the meal some stranger had left for her, she put the fire out, cleaned out the billy and plate and left them on the small rocks at the edge of the fire place, just in case whoever the stranger was decided to come back for them.

She drew the horse close to the fallen tree and was about to mount up when suddenly the same stranger who was at the cave entrance stood close to her and asked if she would allow him to help her. This time she instantly recognised him.

Thank you so much. Yes please help me. Her curiosity fully stirred by now allowed her to ask, was it also you who lit the fire and cooked those beautiful fish and made the tea. Yes Sarsha, remember how I said I would be with you each time you set out to fulfil each part of your journey and all the things that were to be done in connection with every part of that journey?

Well you won't always see me and what I am doing for you, but I felt it was important enough to come and say hello today. Trust me, I will be there with you, even when you can't see me or hear me.

Just remember do not gather large amounts of food to take on your journey I will make sure you always have enough supplies so you can be and do all that I ask of you without fear of going without.

Sarsha travelled for many months through similar countryside. Always finding somewhere to rest of a night, somewhere for horse to graze and always having her food, drink and when necessary having a fire prepared for her before she arrived.

Every time it was done, it was without her seeing or hearing how he did it.

Then one day late in the afternoon, about the time of the evening meal she came over one of the many mountains which she had been previously told about by the stranger. The sun was setting behind the hills and the temperature was dropping quickly.

She came in through a small gap between huge, sharp boulders where there was barely enough space for her and horse. A small building made of wooden slats and a thatched roof appearing to be strong and in good condition was on one side of her. A small dark house which appeared would be blown over with the first gust of wind on the other side.

As she looked around to get her bearings as to where she was, and for someone to ask the name of the village she noticed how cold and dark it was. She saw that it had only one street to the whole village. Many dilapidated houses and some small stores lined both side s of the street. On one side of the street there were only a couple of buildings that barely held together. There stood a strange hill at one end and what appeared to be a castle at the other end. As she was wondering about this and many other questions, a stranger approached her asking; can I help you, you seemed to be lost? Sarsha turned to see who was asking the question and felt that the stranger was somehow familiar but was too tired to work it all out.

Malkendah

Could you please tell me where I am? You are in a village called Malkendah. Can you tell me there is a castle anywhere in this village?

It seems to be too small a place to have any real, good sized castle she thought but I should still ask just in case there is.

If you look down there at the end of the street you will see a castle, it has remained unoccupied for several years now. Why do you want to know about it? Sarsha took out the document and showed it to the stranger.

The stranger smiled but still didn't reveal who he was.

Yes, you are the one to continue with the responsibility and the care of the castle and all that it means. What is your name young lady? I am Sarsha she replied.

I shall let you go now as you need to be inside out of the cold, have a good night's sleep. I shall see you again soon he said and left her to go her way in the direction of the castle that he pointed out.

It was a very short street, she only allowed the horse to walk slowly because of the unknown surrounds and they still reached the castle within a few minutes. She carefully dismounted, took her small bag of clothing which was the only possessions she was told to bring, and released the horse through a side gate close by to the castle, hoping it was in a paddock which belonged to it.

She then tentatively approached the front door way of the castle and attempted to open it, expecting it to be stuck and impossible to open.

She was shocked at how easily and quickly it opened.

Once she entered through the door way she noticed directly in front of her a small candle giving off a soft light, an open fire that smelt wonderful and a small plate of food sitting on the side bricks of the fire place. She knew that the candles she had tucked in among her clothes which she bought with her were obviously going to be of good use here in this place.

Without hesitation she sat down on the floor and began to eat the food which was still hot and tasted strangely beautiful. She turned to place the plate on the floor beside her and bumped the unseen table in the darkness beyond the candle light nearby. So she placed the plate there and took up the goblet of mulled wine which almost fell when she bumped it. She slowly drank that as she thought of all the adventures she had been through to get to this place. Soon her tiredness was more than she wanted to struggle against.

Not knowing where the bedrooms were or if in fact there were any beds with clean blankets or pillows, she simply lay down where she was on the floor and instantly settled into a deep sleep, without moving all night. The fire burned all night and she was as warm as if she had a soft fur rug wrapped around her when she finally stirred in the morning. Early the next morning she awoke to the sound of a multitude of strange birds chattering at her windows. The sun came streaming through in shafts of brilliant light. Momentarily she was disorientated. She rose from the floor and began to look around attempting to make sense of all that surrounded her.

Again not knowing how it got there, she saw some steaming hot food right where she had placed the empty plate the night before. She ate it without too much thought as to where it came from and who cooked it.

The morning sun began to slowly rise in the sky and shine more light around her as it appeared to uncover that which was mysteriously hidden the night before.

Huge pieces of cloth were covering many large objects and this stirred curiosity within Sarsha to investigate straight after she had finished eating.

Still protective towards the few pieces of clothing which she had brought with her, she placed them on top of the small table which she had bumped into the night before.

With the first piece of cloth she removed she was confronted with the first of many and long lasting shocks she would be going through for the many months to follow. There were several huge chairs, the likes of which she had never seen. Carved backs to rest on and the deepest dark brown with tapestry padded seats. A large, highly polished table with hand carved legs, covered with a handmade exquisite tapestry.

After a short time of investigating the room where she was at the time she decided to investigate the rest of the palace, particularly looking for the kitchen. It wasn't long before she found it but couldn't understand why it was so large with cupboards to the ceiling. There was a large wood fire, which was also alight. A kitchen work bench just under a window which opened onto an amazing sight at the back of the palace, of wooded dells with squirrels, rabbits and other small animals scurrying backwards and forwards.,

A large branch from an overgrown tree right at the window had a tiny robin red breast sitting there just watching her. Many other little birds singing their cheerful morning song before they set off for their food as they foraged for scattered seeds and so forth scattered through the huge trees surrounding the castle.

The frost almost melted by now and some straggly flowers gently swaying in the slight breeze turning towards the warmth of the sun.

Sarsha looked thoroughly in many of the cupboards for any food and was surprised to see not one crumb of bread or any other form of food. Then she remembered the words of the stranger that he would supply all that she needed for every part of the journey.

She also remembered that the money steward of the village would be releasing the necessary funds for her needs each time she would go to see him. She saw that there were many other large and strange looking rooms with large, fancy brass, heavily engraved locks on each of them. One of the rooms in particular, which appeared to be more special than the rest of them drew her attention and she nervously approached it. She definitely wanted to enter this room straight away, but then remembered that she had no food or other supplies so decided to do further investigating it later.

After refreshing herself in the basin on the work bench, she changed her clothes and set off to find the money steward, the shops for supply and to see what the rest of the village looked like in the daylight. She wondered if there was some kind of a key to secure her front door and searched for and found it. It lay half hidden under layers of dust which had gathered over the past many years, on the ledge of the window she had just been looking out.

It was a huge brass key, handmade and extensively engraved all over.

As she turned it in the lock she felt the breeze pick up a little more. She heard horse whinnying out to her as it poked its head around the corner of the side paddock.

There was a long track between the house door and the gate which led into the street. It was easy to see that there had been at some time a beautiful garden, but had become so over grown because of the many years of neglect.

From the moment she placed her foot on the pathway outside the gate way she felt the piercing stare of many eyes.

It was quite dark at this end of the street and unusually cold, but she felt perhaps it was only because of the winter season. As she walked further away from the house and began to have a better look at things, she noticed that there was only one street to the whole, tiny village. The village was tucked into the foot hills of a giant mountain which towered overhead like a steel sentinel. From its appearance it looked as if it had become frozen in time.

Whichever way you looked, it was the same in every direction; all you could see were massive mountains towering above everything else in the village, including the tall trees at the back of her castle. There was absolutely no appearance of wealth, warmth or even protection attached to any of these meagre dwellings which were held together by rust, rotten wooden and whatever else they could find to put it together. They had created a semblance of cover over their heads, but many parts of the dwellings could be seen right through from the front to the back as anyone walked past. It was obvious there was no warmth or protection within these structures.

Beyond the village it was easy to see there were many more mountains appearing like wave upon wave of an endless ocean, all towering above this tiny village.

Sarsha could see that where she had just come from, it was in fact a large castle and not just some normal old house which she previously thought the night before. It was right at one end of the village.

As she continued down one side of the street she came to the part where she had entered the village and saw that it was indeed right beside the money steward's place. She entered and showed her papers the stranger had given her. Oh yes, I know who you are lady. I have been told that there is another castle keeper coming to town. I welcome you here and hope your stay will be a good one. Any questions or help you need, just let me know and I will see what I can do for you.

Is it possible to get any large amounts of this in heritance out at any one time sir, Sarsha asked? Only if you have a specific need for it at the time he responded, and then only if it is for the work and care of the castle and the people here in this village. Otherwise you cannot access it at all. Sarsha then remembered the words the stranger had previously spoken in regards to the same thing. They smiled at each other and she left.

When she walked a few steps onto the cobblestone foot path she continued down the same side of the street towards the opposite end of where she had just come from and soon came to a tiny, single fronted shop which would have not drawn a second glance if she had seen it anywhere else.

The Village Weaver

Apparently it had not drawn a second glance of value from any of the locals either.

No one could ever remember seeing it being repaired, painted or maintained in any manner at any time.

Although it was always basically clean looking, at least on the outside, none the less it was still rather drab looking as far as they were concerned.

The old women of the village had nothing more than a few critical comments to make about it, such as; why there were no plants, and there really doesn't appear to be much life about the dull old place.

Why weren't there at least a few trees close to it to give some shade in the heat of the day? On and on their negative words tumbled from their mouths before they had ever stopped to think of what they were saying.

So then who would want to go anywhere near such a place which had no form of outward beauty or appeal to the natural eyes?

However, no one had taken the time to go and look or ask questions to find out what it was all about.

The one or two who previously had any interest at all were too afraid to do anything about it, because they were incredibly concerned about being cut off from the rest of the villagers if they had dared to go beyond the opinion of the majority.

The only person who had been seen coming or going from the shop was a rather plain looking man approximately thirty five, who also had no outward appearance of beauty or appeal of any kind. Still, no one had taken the time to talk to him and get to know him either.

It was never known where he had come from or what his life was about. But they did have the time to think and suggest to each other, that from their judgement that he had to be some kind of strange person, maybe a criminal or even worse.

Sarsha wanted to get her cleaning and foods supplies and begin the cleanup of her new home. Because of that she felt to leave it till another time before she investigated the shop for herself, but her curiosity had been seriously, deeply stirred again.

As she turned to look for a place to buy her food and cleaning supplies, she noticed that there were not many shops at all in the street. It was easy to see how short the street was and how miserable the few, tiny, rundown buildings appeared.

Now she could also clearly see the building she had come out of at the beginning of the day, where she had slept the night before was in fact the largest castle she could have imagined, and suddenly realised, this was indeed the main reason she had come to the village in the first place. It was a strange looking place even to her; in fact it looked just as strange to her as the tiny shop and the castle did to the villagers for a long time. She wondered if perhaps that could be a good talking point with the villagers later, as she attempted to get to know them better.

The continued tide of negative, idle comments about these two strange and unwanted buildings had persisted since the village became known as a cold and dark place many years beforehand.

Still their thoughts persisted; why these two places were there at all, who took care of them, and who lived there. Yes, and still no one took the time or courage to investigate and find out the truth of the matter and to see if they could do anything about it.

One or two thought at some time that they had occasionally seen a lone woman walking around in the gardens that surrounded the castle, but they could not remember how long ago that was. Some even seemed to vaguely remember that they had seen a woman sitting for long hours with her head bent low with nothing more than the light of a flickering candle around her. No one knew or could say who had lived there before her, neither could they remember how long before Sarsha came had anyone else had lived there.

Of course they asked all the same things as they would have about any new arrival.

Why was she there? Where did she come from? Did she have any family and where did she live beforehand. However they only ever asked this among themselves and never from Sarsha herself.

Though they were not prepared to approach Sarsha herself they remained suspicious of her and continued to judge her harshly from every angle.

After all they often commented, who does she think she is? Why does she have to have such a fancy place all to herself and not a smaller cottage which is far better and more appropriate place like ours? It had never entered their mind to ask or even consider that she may have had something of any value that she may have wanted to share with them.

It had definitely never entered their mind that perhaps she may have wanted to have some normal interaction with them instead of being constantly on her own in the big and lonely castle.

Sarsha had always been interested in different nationalities and the cultures, foods and customs with the wonderful sounds of all the different languages. She was finding it quite difficult however this time to get to know this new group of people in this tiny, strange village.

Early each morning Sarsha would take a walk down one side of the street which ran down the whole length of the village, stop momentarily in front of the small fronted shop, turn around and walk back up the other side which was filled with an appearance of tall, dark rocks, and back home again to her castle.

Many times she would stop at one or two gateways and chat for a short while. She could never bear the thought of anyone going cold. She had known far too many times herself what it was like to go cold with hunger like a ravenous wolf howling at the door way.

She had spent many of her years as a child hungry and cold with not enough clothing to wear or shoes on her feet. She could not remember the amount of times she had to walk many kilometres to school without shoes on her feet and how they had became quite painful and half frozen on the rough and badly made roads.

Sarsha remembered well how most of her nights of the past were spent being awake as she shivered and shook with the intense cold during the winter months. But then, none of her family had enough blankets to keep them, warm either.

Like many families of that era they did not have enough clothing or food to keep them warm through the day let alone try to wear some extra to stay warm of a night time.

So many times she simply wanted to die to escape the cold and the hunger gnawing at her stomach. She always waited for the morning to come with great anticipation, looking forward to what she may be able to do to take her mind off her emptiness. Sometimes of a day time she would run through any nearby fields or walk and talk with the cows who came up to investigate the small one who dared to enter their paddock.

Sometimes she simply sat and listened to the many small birds chattering away in the nearby trees. Sometimes she would swim in the nearest water way regardless to its depth. She was never afraid of the water or any of its possible but unknown dangers. Sometimes, she would try to catch as many as possible of the many, varied insects which often covered the large trees in the bush around where her family lived.

She remembered all these things which remained with her even after she became married and had her own children.

She knew what it was like when her own children did not have enough warm clothing to wear or enough healthy food to eat from time to time. But she also knew it would never be as bad as when she was a child and what it was like in her part of the world at that time.

Of course much had happened in Sarshas life since that time.

She was so proud of the life that her children had made for themselves as they grew up. Their courage and commitment to work hard and live good lives and still enjoy life constantly made her heart swell with pride. But Sarsha could never free herself of the awful memories of what it was really like for so long in the past with so much hunger and coldness and knew she must learn to keep it to herself and not cause others to worry.

Not long after all her children had grown up and left home, and her husband had died, she had a strange visitor who came to visit her from a far away strange country.

She hesitantly invited him in and they sat to have some of her homemade soup and some light hearted chatter.

He had presented her with many legal documents for her to read and consider carefully and then sign. He would be seeing her again the next day.

Soon after he quietly arose and left without another word.

It was many hours before she could clearly think of any of his specific comments, especially all the fancy words and legal jargon that seemed to roll around inside her head like metal balls crashing together.

Eventually she put some more wood on the fire and settled down for the night warmly snuggled under the warmest blankets she could imagine.

She began to read the many papers the stranger has left behind for her to examine and fell asleep half way through the process.

Excuse me lady, the words came crashing through her private thoughts, are you alright the stranger asked? Suddenly Sarsha realised she was indeed standing still in the middle of the street with many other strangers watching her. She knew the loneliness of this village had caused her to start wandering back to the past in her thoughts and was thinking if anything much had really changed for the better in her life.

I must keep going, I must keep going and complete all that is involved in my reason to be in this village she told herself.

Still I am amazed at the incredible differences of which I live in now. I have all the food I need, all the great clothing already made and fitting perfectly. Anybody would think they were made and designed for me specifically. A garden in which I can do anything I like. I live in the biggest possible castle anyone could imagine and I no longer have to pay any rent for it. I have all the beautiful and warm blankets I need and many to spare as well. I never have to go cold again or wear filthy dirty rags which don't fit properly and which make me look like some street urchin. I no longer have to wear left off clothing from anyone else who were simply sick of wearing them. Hand me downs are no longer a part of my life. She was yet to discover the garments left behind from her grandmother in the large cupboards.

She then quietly continued her walk back to the castle. When she arrived back at the castle and carefully stored all her supplies, her curiosity quickly increased and strengthened to the point that she felt unable to begin the cleaning and organising of the place.

She did however begin to investigate the rest of the huge rooms and was continually impressed with the fact that all the doors had huge brass handles and locks on each of them. She wondered where all the keys were and decided to try the key that had opened and locked the front door. She was surprised and happy to see that the one key opened every door that she tried. As she continued to investigate the vast place she saw yet another door that she had not previously noticed. Her attention was drawn to the intricate detail of the heavy carving on the door. Then realised that each door she came to had the exact same carving on each of them and stood there in amazement at the beauty of the work. This room though it was like all the rest, tightly closed by a large brass handle and lock, it was quickly opened with one turn of the brass key and she entered wondering what hidden secrets or treasures it may hold. There right in front of her stood the most beautiful cupboards, all with the same kind of engraving as the door ways to each room. She nervously approached one of them and tried the same key which opened each door way of each room and was delighted to see how quickly and easily it opened this cupboard as well. She felt perhaps each door that she opened seemed to be easier that the one before but did not stop long enough to think about it in any depth, she just wanted to start looking into what was behind every door.

Sarsha cried aloud in surprise, there to her utter amazement on one of the many shelves was one of the most beautiful crowns that she could have ever imagined or even described.

It had large natural pearls along the front and at the sides which shimmered in the sunlight. There were rubies set into the sides of it as well. Then right in the centre front was the largest and most beautiful amethyst Sarsha had ever seen or heard of. I suppose this is what they call the crown Jewells she thought.

She soon discovered the other cupboards in that room had the royal jewels and royal gowns which the last queen had worn when she held court, especially on the significant occasions of importance to the villagers.

Sarsha took out some of the garments and left all the jewels and the crown where they were and locked the cupboard again. She believed that day she probably would never wear the crown but that she would keep it to look at occasionally to remind her of the awesome responsibility she had to deal with in the upkeep of the castle and the care of the villagers.

She then left and locked the room again and busied herself in the cleaning and organising of the castle so as to bring it back into a fully functional and safe place of good order.

She also took some time to check out if there was any kind of a garden surrounding where she lived. She did so and found a vast place looking much like a miniature jungle at the back of her castle. She began to make plans to make the surrounding grounds into a place of visible order and obvious beauty.

Several weeks went by as she steadily worked alone at the preparation of bringing herself and her new home into readiness for the rest of her life's journey and work.

She did not seek any help because she did not feel she knew the villagers well enough to ask them for assistance, and no one had come to offer her a hand or talk to her either. They were still too afraid and too suspicious to do so.

Finally she was happy enough to settle down to making some more warm clothes for the local people. She began to feel quite lonely but continued all day and often into the dark hours of the night. She found that the memories of her past days and nights of cold and hunger wouldn't allow her to give up her passion to provide for others. She began to think about the first time as she sat down to begin the garments. She was still overcome by how much incredible material she found in some of the cupboards in one of the many large rooms. She knew that the bounty of material and the obvious quality of it all would continue to influence her approach and quality of work with each garment. She knew there was no longer any material made anywhere which could match the quality, strength and beauty of what was in that place at her disposal and in her control.

Often she would put down her sewing and sit wondering for a while, wondering if the day would come when she could she could go and sit amongst some really good friends. She wondered about sharing at least some of the pain of the past.

She would have been just as happy however to have shared perhaps some of the good things and fine memories, for she knew that not all of the things of the past were bad.

Each time of resting only lasted a short while then she would become busy again making her fine garments.

Sarsha did have great confidence in making fine garments, but seriously lacked confidence in making new friends in a new and strange place.

One morning as she woke up with the sun filtering through the small opening where the curtains met. It filled her room before she had pulled back the heavy curtains which covered her windows. As she pulled them back and saw how bright the day was her heart filled with renewed confidence that this was the day to start giving to the villagers the garments which she had made over many months. The sun was quite warm and Sarshas heart filled with happiness, and a sense of well being the like of which she hadn't had for some time. But there was still a residue coldness which lingered deep within her which she found hard to shake off. Sarsha wondered just how long it would be before she would be totally free of those haunting memories of long ago, memories of the cold and the sounds of hunger snarling like a wolf at her door. She did know for sure though that each time they surfaced again that they were softening and receding more and more each time.

The flowers in her garden smelt so beautiful that day. The little birds flitted from flower to flower and from tree to tree as they burst out with their cheerful, beautiful and sometimes strange songs which seemed never ending. From some of the stories which had been passed down by word of mouth through the many generations of the village, there had apparently been many different kinds of beautiful kinds, far more than there had been for a long time now though. Their bright colours reminded her of some of the more colourful garments which she had been making. So she went to her special cupboard where she stored her hand made clothing and filled the largest basket she could find with as many garments as possible.

She then went to the room where she had placed some of her royal gowns and chose one which was as bright as the birds and flowers in the garden outside.

She had hoped that it would cover up the residue coldness she still felt inside and that it would make her appear bright and happy to everyone she spoke to.

Finally she closed the large front door and started to walk down one side of the village street.

Because it was a bit warmer than it had been for some time and that there was nothing better for them to do, the villagers were outside at the front of their houses chatting to one another as their children played on the road nearby. The little ones were running and laughing as if the whole world was made just for them and that no one and nothing else existed beyond their tiny village.

Most of them had no shoes on their feet. The clothing on their little backs were nothing more than dirty scraps of cloth which barely held together and which certainly didn't cover them well or keep them warm.

Most of the mothers had the same scraps of rags on their backs and their bodies were nothing more than bones covered with wrinkled skin.

Sarsha had learnt through much reading and from scraps of information she was able to glean from some of the shop keepers that most of the men and the fathers of the village were no longer around. They had either been killed in the many wars which they went out to fight in an effort to protect their own and surrounding villages, or they had been so badly injured or traumatised that they were unable to find their way back home. Many of the men had gone to other villages and places beyond their own area to find work and get provisions for their families. Some had gone somewhere beyond the tall mountains surrounding the village. But none of them ever came back.

This left only a few old men who were unable to be of much help to the women and children left behind. These men were hardly ever seen outside but their muffled voices came drifting to the front of their drab cottages and could be heard when the cold winds were blowing from behind them. Most of the men, women and children had died from starvation through the bitter cold winters which often ravaged the tiny village.

Many a time the wild ones as they were called, who came from a far away country beyond the mountains came in raiding parties. Nobody could understand the strange language that they spoke, or where they came from or where they went when they left the village. For centuries this was the pattern of life for that tiny village. These marauders came and went as they pleased and no one was able to predict when they would come or why they came or where they went when they left. There was never anything of any real value they took with them, but none the less it was still total destruction left behind each time they left the village.

One by one Sarsha went from house to house attempting to talk to some of the mothers, occasionally stopping to talk to some of the children and play with them. Mostly they were suspicious of this stranger who dared to come close to them and their children and yelled at her to go away and leave them alone. On the odd occasion one of the women would invite her in to have a drink or share some morsel of food. She could see how poor they all were and yet how willing one or two were to share what they had despite their own desperate need.

This was a real shock to Sarsha to see just how free and joyous they were to share their meagre supplies.

Whenever she was permitted to, she gave one or two garments to the family where she was visiting.

Sometimes, the ones who received the garments wanted to pay her for them because they felt they had been brought from some other world and they certainly didn't want to be indebted to anyone. They were afraid of what may be required of them later if they accepted the clothing too readily. They had never seen or heard about such beautiful material or seen such colours, or known clothing could be made with such unusual designs. Somehow this clothing didn't seem real to them at all.

They couldn't believe or understand why Sarsha would not allow them to pay for the clothing.

After a period of time of this chatting and offering the clothing as she walked down the street some of the villagers were happy enough to allow her to be visiting whenever she wanted. Even fewer offered her a drink or a morsel to eat on the rare occasion. However bit by bit they began to trust her to speak to and play with their children, but they still suspiciously watched her each time. Some others however would watch her walk near then pretend they did not see her and turn their backs and not speak as she came nearer. On many occasion this particular group would spit words of venom at her as she walked by. After all, who did she think she was, how could such a rich looking lady with such fancy clothing, make such expensive garments and just give them away for nothing, what was she after?

For a short time, a few of the villagers appeared to be happy enough to be her friends as she walked down the village street, as long as she didn't come too close or look them in the eye whenever she would attempt to talk to them. Still no one ever attempted to go and see her in her big castle at the other end of the street.

For many months Sarsha kept on making those wonderful garments, each one a little better than the one before. Each one from the vast and rich supply of materials she found in the cupboards. The whole time she was trying to make them better and better. But her main aim all the time was simply for the people to have some beautiful clothing to keep them warm and for them to know she really did care about them.

She could clearly see there were not very many people in that small village, there was even less money for the people to buy materials to make their own garments, repair houses, grow a garden or run some live stock.

Little by little some of the mothers continued to relax more and actually enjoy her company without being quite as suspicious of her.

Nivek And His Pupp

One day as Sarsha set off to have a quiet walk down the street simply enjoying the warmth of the sun and the sounds of the little birds, without trying to give any garments to any of the families, she saw a small boy running backwards and forwards across the street directly in front of her. A tiny puppy had been following him every step of the way, wagging its tail and stopping to lick the boys hand each time he stopped.

She attempted to follow the boy and his puppy calling out to them many times. They appeared not to hear her. The boy never spoke and the puppy never allowed her to touch it either. She became curious about both of them and felt she had never seen either of them before during the many times she had been up and down the street. She did however have a haunting sense of something familiar about the boy in the back of her mind. So she began to enquire with some of the villagers if they knew where they had come from. They were only mildly curious as to where the boy and the dog came from or where they lived now, but still not curious enough to do anything about it.

They were however highly critical as to the boys appearance which was even more raggedy than their own children. They had hardly noticed the lack of clothing of their own children and their dirty appearance, but none the less felt they had the right to their critical judgement of the apparent dirt of the little boy. No one had seen them before or had any idea where they had come from.

All they knew was that a couple of days before they had heard a dog yapping and that they had all gone outside to see what it was, because as far as they could remember,none of them had owned any kind of animal, let alone a dog, therefore the noise was strange and something that challenged and frightened them.

Finally she decided to return home and spend some time in the sunshine as she continued with more of the work that was badly needed to bring the garden into the kind of place she would be happy to invite someone into to share it with her.

Late that afternoon she realised she hadn't eaten all day and set about to have something to eat. It wasn't long before she realised she was actually looking for the little puppy at her back door. She had hoped that by some miracle of a chance it and the little boy may have followed her home. Considering the fact that no one in the village knew where they come from, perhaps they would be happy enough to stay with her. She looked but nothing was there.

Disappointment flooded her heart and she couldn't shake the feeling of some great loss, though she didn't understand why.

After dark as she settled into the warmth and comfort of her beautiful blankets and tried to sleep she became even more restless. Every time she attempted to close her eyes all she could see were the big brown eyes of the puppy and the broad smile on the little boys face.

She continued to feel as though she recognised the boys face from somewhere a long time ago, but the fog in her mind swirled so thick and covered the memory, she couldn't remember anything clearly.

Exhaustion caused her finally to fall asleep in the early hours of the morning. She was awoken by the sounds of some child crying. As she stirred and rose to see who it was, she was shocked to realise the sobbing and crying was actually coming from her own mouth and this frightened her. She sat down suddenly on the side of the bed until the crying ceased and then quickly got dressed. She lit the fire and sat there watching the light flicker across her bedroom as the flames danced with vigour. Her mind kept returning to the joy and energy which the puppy and boy had. Were they hungry she thought, where did they live, and with so little clothing was the boy ever cold? She could see the puppy running to and fro across her mind as the smiling boy seemed to be beckoning her to come and follow him.

The days were getting colder all the time now and Sarsha became busier still with making as many clothes as possible for the villagers.

This was her routine for many weeks with the nagging ache in the depth of her heart as to when she could hold the boy and the puppy as well as where did they live and were they alright for food and shelter. Night after night with her fire going and the great hall of her castle alight as she continued her work. She was oblivious to the fact there was a stranger constantly watching her through the large windows as he stood at the gate way of the castle.

Many times she would be going to bed as the sun began to rise and the villagers were gathering once again at their gate ways for the usual daily chatter. After one of those late nights she was only asleep for what seemed a few moments and she was awoken with an unusual bird song. She sat up suddenly not with fear but with the surprise of such a delightful sound that she had never heard before. She slowly walked to the large window and there sitting on a branch tip which almost touched her window was the reddest robin she could have imagined. A new visitor to the place she thought aloud. Then she noticed several others sitting a little higher in the tree. Oh this is surely a day for new things to be happening she mused. It's great that those little strangers feel comfortable about coming here and sitting so close to my window. Then her mind started to flood again with thoughts of the little boy and the puppy's face and the fact that they always seemed to be bursting with joy.

Sarsha knew she would continue to look for the puppy and the boy and hopefully get to hug both of them one day and find out where they had come from. Maybe she could also find out why they seemed to cause such a sense of loss deep within her whenever she thought about them.

After some breakfast of hot tea and dried biscuits she loaded up her basket with some of the warm clothing, locked up the front door to the castle and set off yet again to walk down the street with high hopes of being able to share some of the garments without upsetting the villagers.

Sarsha struggled with her emotions which ran between wanting to share the clothing with the villagers who must have been close to freezing and finding the boy and the puppy which she wanted so dearly to hold close to her. She determined to concentrate on the villagers and not be pulled apart with what may never happen.

For some unexplainable reason Sarsha had felt to put on the most regal and the most expensive looking gown which sparkled with all the gemstones which were sewn on it. As soon as she left the gate, horse whinnied at her and some of the birds from the back of the castle came rushing towards her with an unusually excited burst of song. Sarsha felt as though they were trying to tell her something but she didn't understand at all.

Only a few steps down the path way and there they were again, the little boy running and laughing as the puppy followed him with a few excited yelps as the boy patted him and stroke his fur. For a short time they were actually closer to her than they had been before whenever they ran down the street. She called and called to them but they appeared not to hear her. She was hurt and puzzled as to why they were acting this way. After all, all that she wanted to do was to share some of their joy and apparent closeness. This time she followed all the way and was right behind them as they ran right down to the other end of the street.

Sarsha then forgot about everything else and had actually begun to run after them. The faster she ran the faster they ran but the distance between them had quickly closed. But not enough for her to catch them before they entered the shop with the narrow front which no one could tell why it was there. None of the villagers had had enough interest to enter the shop and find out what it was about. They only considered it to be an unnecessary, ugly place of no worth and that it should be removed.

Suddenly she was now at the door way of the small fronted shop, but the puppy and the boy had run into the shop, with the little boy instantly disappearing. She quickly followed behind into the shop before she realised she had done so. For a few moments the puppy ran around her feet then it too just disappeared. Where have they gone she thought?

Sarsha Meets Manuel

Can I help you lady came the same sweet voice she had heard a long time ago at the mouth of the cave. Sarsha was shocked and she spun around to see a stranger coming towards her, at the same time dropping her basket full of the warm clothing on the floor. At that point she saw what had once been a gorgeous gown now looking raggedy and ugly as it hung on her all wet. It was now hanging like an old rag on her body and she was devastated to see just how bad it really did look. Oh no she groaned my gown my beautiful gown what will I do with it now, this is one thing I don't know how to fix and make it look better. I will have to go home straight away and change into something dry and warm. She looked for the man which had spoken to her all those years ago but couldn't see him. Can I help you he asked again? She could only see yet another stranger standing before her. Who is he and what does he want she wondered.

You are all wet; here sit here till your clothes are dried by the warm fire. I am not wet she snapped. It is sunny outside. Come over here he said and see for yourself, it is now actually raining quite heavily. As the stranger continued to speak gently to her he was able to persuade her to stay at least for a short while. Finally she sat in the large chair near the fire place. Somehow it looked quite similar to the main one back at the castle which was the throne. It looked hard and very uncomfortable. She was surprised at just how comfortable it was however once she sat down. Her mind was now trying to remember just when it was that it had started to rain.

Sarsha was embarrassed to see such heavy rain and to realise she had not noticed when it had began. She decided to accept the offer of a time by the fire but was hesitant about it though. Would you like a warm drink while you are waiting? Again she hesitantly accepted the offer and could not say why she did so. The soft spoken words coming from the stranger were soothing her fears and she began to feel she had no legitimate argument to refuse his kind offer. It seemed to be only a few fleeting moments when the stranger brought the drink to her, she noticed it was in a similar gold goblet to those which she found at the castle amongst the things which she assumed were for guests when there were special occasions happening there. Perhaps they were used at times of the queen holding court with matters regarding the sovereignty of her responsibility for the village and the villagers.

That goblet is truly beautiful she exclaimed, look at the shine on it, and look at the gems encrusted all around it and oh even the tray it is on has the same kind of jewels encrusted in the edge all around it. It must have cost a great deal of money. Sarsha seriously questioned in her mind as to whether she was worthy enough to hold such a fine piece of work let alone actually be allowed to drink from it. Then she realised she had been quite rude with the rushing of questions and fell silent for a few moments in her embarrassment. As she held the cup and began to drink, it tasted a little like honey in milk with cinnamon in it but as she looked at it she saw that it was clear like red wine. Though she did not know what it was, she felt safe and confident enough to drink it. She still felt too embarrassed to ask what it was so sat there silently wondering. The stranger knew exactly what she wanted to know so he explained that it was in fact milk. Sarsha had drank milk many, many times before and it had not looked like or tasted like what she was now holding in her hands. Yes that is right he commented in response to her unspoken thoughts. Now she was a little frightened, if he could know her thoughts could he also place harmful thoughts into her mind that would harm her? Again he responded to her unspoken words I shall never harm you or give you thoughts or anything that will harm you or cause you to harm others with.

There are many other ingredients of superior value in that milk. They are things which you cannot yet begin to comprehend, but you will fully understand one day Sarsha. He then explained to Sarsha how he got the milk fresh each day from the cows which his father had kept on the mountains directly behind the shop. Sarsha realised she had never noticed any of the huge mountains before but could clearly see them now through the window near the fire place, as the stranger continued to speak.

After a few more minutes the stranger asked Sarsha if she would like to change her gown and put on a new one. Only then did she see what it was that the stranger had been working on the whole time she was there, except for the few brief moments he took to get her the lovely hot drink. It was the most beautiful gown she had seen. Its luminous beauty and incredible design far exceeded anything that was in any of the locked cupboards at home in the castle. Nothing could have prepared her thoughts for the beauty of the garment which the stranger was holding out in front of him towards her now.

She was puzzled and still a little frightened, after all why did this stranger want to give her something so beautiful and so expensive looking. Suddenly she began to have some idea of what some of the villagers were going through when she first tried to present the beautiful garments to them. Even though the gown which she now wore and owned was nowhere near as beautiful as the one now being presented to her, she still wanted to keep it. After all it was left to her by her great grandmother. Everything became a little too much for her to handle she was frightened now. She stood up in such a hurry that she dropped the golden goblet and banged her leg on the side of the chair which now appeared to be the ugliest chair she had ever seen. I am confused she thought. The drink was beautiful, every drop of it made me feel stronger, and strangely alive. She could still hear the words ringing in her ears, thank you sir, it is a wonderful drink and in such a special goblet. Had I really spoken them she wondered.

After a short while she attempted to go home again, but you are still all wet the stranger commented. Wouldn't you like to change your gown before you get a chill? No sir, I am fine in what I am wearing. Her pride did not allow her to accept such a personal offer from a man and certainly not from a stranger. She hurriedly made a grab for her basket and the fallen goblet as her pride continued to rise up like a fire in her heart. She could not control her embarrassment as she quickly moved towards the door and attempted to leave. She almost knocked the stranger over as she rushed toward the door. Only then did she remember the puppy that she had originally came to enquire about. It was now outside, yapping at the door of the shop. She went to hand back the goblet to the stranger but he stepped back a little and said, Sarsha don't you want to take the goblet with you too. It's not mine she snapped. The stranger continued with his calm sweet words, actually that belongs to you, if you look closely at the side where your hands cover it you will see that your own name is engraved there" Sarsha quickly shoved the goblet into the stranger's hand and as she did so she saw clearly that her name was engraved on its side. She was shocked to see the stranger had told the truth. In shock she dropped it again and ran out of the shop.

Wait, wait just a moment the stranger softly pleaded with a slight touch of urgency in his voice. Don't be afraid. Sarsha stopped in her steps and stared at him wondering what was coming next. Won't you please change out of your wet gown and into this one made especially for you? Also I really want you to keep the golden goblet; it was made especially for you, no one else is ever going to drink from it. No, no she cried in fear and then ran out the door. Much to her surprise, half way down the street she noticed again the boy and the little pup where still there. But they would still not allow her to touch them. Her thoughts were racing now about what had just happened at the shop with the stranger and she wanted to desperately escape the sense of a loss of control, or at least work out what was happening. Her mind was now in total turmoil for her thoughts were racing between how she wanted to hold the boy and the puppy, and the uncertainty of stepping into anything else that would shake her control over what was happening around her. She was now at the gate way of the palace and realised it had not been raining since she left the door way of the strange little shop. The rain had stopped and the sun was sweeping across the street causing each puddle to glisten like diamonds.

So she tried to ignore the boy and his happy companion. She ignored a few of the villagers as they waved to her. She ignored horse as it whinnied at her as she entered the gate of the castle. She ignored the sweet songs of the birds as they flitted from branch to branch on the trees and plants which had been recently weeded and trimmed. But she could not ignore that gnawing sense that she knew the voice of the stranger in the shop and the face of the little boy, even though she didn't at that time know where from. As she put the basket with the garments still in it on the floor near her bed, she saw how drenched they had become from being open to the rain. Sarsha knew she would have to take her time and work carefully to be able to present them to the villagers later. Then she looked down at the way the beautiful gown now hung like a cheap rag on her body. In her anxiety she hurriedly tried to take it off her and badly tore it in many places in the process. She sat there on her bed sobbing uncontrollably at she realised the destruction of such an incredible gown was now beyond all repair. She knew her limited skills made it impossible for her to re make the gown or even repair such damage. The loss of something so precious which she had only worn once was more than she could bear. Once more her pride stopped her thoughts from even contemplating that someone else may have been able to help her fix it. If she couldn't fix it then no one else could either. She fell asleep on the bed and only awoke as her stomach began to rumble with hunger. She had forgotten the fact that she had not put the gown away, she could see it was no longer in her hands and assumed she had dealt with it before she fell asleep though she could not really remember what she actually did with it

After some hearty lunch she decided to simply sit and relax out in the garden at the back of her palace. The first thought that came to mind at that point was the fact that after the first two days of being in the castle the fire was no longer lit for her before she got out of bed. She also realised that there were no longer meals being prepared and left for her by the stranger.

She wondered about that, and then realised that once she found where the wood was and that she knew well how to start a fire, no one had to do it for her. She recognised also that once she had started to utilise the pension that was left for her to buy food and things necessary for the care of the castle, she no longer needed the unusual supply of food and meals which had been supplied to her for a time, and always by a stranger.

Again the small birds came closer and closer to her and sang their little hearts out to her. She began to imagine she heard words like don't worry, just relax, wait and see, good things are about to begin to happen that are beyond all your wildest imaginations.

She fell asleep in the warmth of the sun as it rested gently on her shoulders. When the sun had set and the night air began to settle in she awoke and went inside totally at peace realising she could now keep up with her thoughts. I shall go again tomorrow, she spoke aloud, down that street and see if I can find the boy and the puppy.

She enjoyed a good night's sleep and awoke earlier than usual the following morning. But this time she did not light the fire as normal. She had a sense of urgency about finding the puppy and boy. She dressed hurriedly, again in one of the sumptuous gowns which had been left in the great cupboards. This one too glowed with the unusual colours and the many gems which were sewn on it. Even if I can't understand what is happening with some of these strange things going on around me she pondered, at least the simple villagers will think I am in control of my life and its strange circumstances which are happening more often lately. At least they will think that I look like a real queen. Surely they will admire me and want to spend more time with me then, maybe even want to visit me at the castle some day.

As she left the gateway again, horse whinnied at her and though she was lost in her thoughts she stopped to stroke his snout and gently pat him on the side of the face.

Some of the birds from the back garden came again and sang their beautiful songs for her. She had not noticed any butterflies in the garden before, but now there was an iridescent blue one sitting on her shoulder and tears of delight filled her eyes at the sight of something so beautiful being so close to her. For a few moments the beauty of the butterfly had diverted her attention from what she thought was beautiful beyond measure in the gown that she was wearing.

As she moved down the foot path the butterfly left her shoulder and flew to the back of the castle. Some of the villagers were as usual standing at their front gate way and one or two smiled at her and waved singing out as she walked past," where did you get such a beautiful gown I have never seen anything like it before. She felt pleased about that, for finally she felt she was able to walk down the street and receive open recognition because of the apparent wealth she was able to wear on her back. Sarsha was so enveloped with the villager's comments that she hadn't noticed that it had begun to rain again. Her excitement about maybe catching up with the puppy and the boy kept her moving forwards towards the other end of the street. She noticed the puppy and boy just a few steps down the foot path in front of her and she noticed that day they seemed to be closer than ever before. Oh she felt that this time she would be able to hold both of them. But not so, they ran always just ahead of her, and occasionally ran back towards her and even around her but still not allowing her to touch them. She did not notice this time either that indeed it had begun to rain quite heavily. Finally at the front of the strange shop the boy disappeared and the puppy ran straight into the shop and out through the back of it as she followed closes behind. Only then did she notice that her gown was hanging drably on her body because of the heavy downpour as she came down the street.

Before she had the time to cry with disappointment because of another ruined gown and become frustrated, she heard the words,

"Hello Sarsha." Again she heard that same soft voice. Oh no she thought, what is happening. That same voice yet it is the face of a stranger. As she turned she saw many beautiful gowns on a bench nearby and the colours appeared to be floating around them. She forcibly tried to control her emotions this time and determined not to show fear or any form of being out of control in her actions and words.

Would you like to sit by the fire and dry off he offered? Yes please she replied. Would you also like to have something warm to drink? That would be nice she responded. He was only gone for a few seconds and he had brought back the same goblet with the jewels and her engraved name on the side of it in one hand. In his other hand there was a plate with the same kind of jewels all around the sides and some food on it. Draped over that same arm that carried the plate of food, he carried the same gown that he had offered her the last time she was in the shop. She accepted the food without questioning this time. She was delighted to taste the meat and how it was cooked was a real surprise to her. She thought it was a little bit unusual to see many figs at the side of the meat and to taste them was better than anything she had experienced before.

Would you like to change out of your wet gown and put this dry warm one on. Sarsha noticed that it was indeed the same one she saw last time and though it was quite beautiful. Still, she did not want to lose control of the one she had chosen herself from her treasures from the locked cupboards? You can keep your own as well he exclaimed. Or you can leave it here for me to clean and dry for you.

If you like you can change your gown over in that small room at the side of the bench.

Sarsha began to feel warm and safe but still struggled a little with someone other than herself even suggesting to put on a gown which she hadn't chosen. Well she thought I am still able to change into my own gown later if I want, I may as well give it a try with this new thing which is being presented to me. She placed the goblet with the remains of her drink on the bricks at the aide of the fire place to keep warm while she changed into this new gown. As she entered the little room the stranger showed her where the lock was if she wanted to use it to make her feel safer. She closed the door behind her and noticed it was made of the same fine brass as the handles on the doors at home in her castle.

When she finally put the new, dry gown on she gasped with delight. It was far more beautiful than any of her gowns locked up at home in the cupboards and far more beautiful than any of the ones she had ever made herself.

She could not imagine why a stranger would want to give her anything so beautiful and not want to be payed for it.

When she came out of the room she was still gently sobbing, she handed her wet gown to the stranger and said you may as well use this in the making of some of the gowns for other people. He silently accepted it and carefully placed it on the end of the bench where the other gowns were.

She quietly and carefully sat down again near the fire in the same old chair that she had been sitting in before. As she put her hand on the chair to steady herself she felt what she thought there were cracks in it. As she had a closer look, the light from the fire showed in greater detail than she had previously noticed what amazing work was involved in the carving of it. It was covered in the same beautiful and unusual patterns as the throne in the castle. As she then stooped to pick up her drink again she remembered the man that was quietly sitting there. He had been patiently waiting for her to become more comfortable in his presence. She drank more of the warm milk, put her cup down then looked up at the stranger with tears in her eyes.

Who are you she asked and why are you being so kind to someone you don't even know, and how come this gown fits me so perfectly as if it was made just for me?

I am Manuel Sarsha. Why are you worried about me being kind to you? Don't you want to be treated kindly and with special care? Don't you want someone to be giving you good things especially the things which you need?

The reason the gown fits so well, is because it was actually made especially for you. But, she stammered, how did you know what size to make it and what if I had never accepted it from you? What would have happened to it then?

Manuel didn't speak for a few moments. He silently arose and went and got another cup of that special milk. As he handed it to her he began to speak to her about how he had been watching her every day as she had walked up and down the street giving those beautiful garments to the villagers. You think you have never seen me before in this village, before you followed the boy and his puppy into my shop that first day, but Sarsha I have seen you every day.

I watched you all those times as you tried so hard to get the little boy to talk to you and as you tried to touch the puppy.

I saw how sad you were, each time as you walked away without them noticing you were even there as you thought.

I watched you as you closed that big door every time you walked alone into that large castle where you live at the other end of the street.

I have seen your lights on every night, many hours after all the other people had turned theirs off.

What did you do in those hours Sarsha?

Did you cry in those hours or did you make all those beautiful garments which I have seen you giving so many times to the villagers. Were you lonely, did you think much about how no one had ever come to see you in the castle, even though you tried to let them know you cared about how they felt when they were so cold and hungry?

Were you ever happy Sarsha, or are there only the things that you thought about in those many, many hours as you sat with your lights on night after night which made you sad?

Sarsha your gown fits you so perfectly because I have woven the material and made gowns for many, many years and I know exactly what size fits each person and what suits them best.

It was so strange to hear Manuel talk to her like this. She now believed that somehow he really did care about her after all, why he would take so much notice of what she had been doing for so long.

She hung her head and cried for a long time before she could open her mouth and talk to Manuel again. As she wiped the tears from her eyes the colour of her gown seemed clearer than it appeared before.

It was a strange type of material and the colours were like a shiny rainbow. Yet in different ways as she turned she saw that the gown was indeed only white and was made of the most exquisite handmade lace she had ever seen.

Again she found it hard to talk calmly and clearly yet she still found enough strength to ask some further questions.

Manuel, why and how did you make it so beautiful, surely it must have taken a very long time to make.

Yes it did take a long time to make he told her and I had to go to far away countries to find the right kind of silk threads, bring it home and weave it for you along with all the other gowns for the other women that would one day need special garments. Manuel explained how necessary it was to search so carefully and to have taken such special care for the gowns. This was needed especially when they were going to be used so often and possibly ruined by getting wet or simply when they wore out if they were made carelessly and without the best possible quality materials. Oh Sarsha cried, will this one wear out Manuel. No he responded it will never wear out and it will never fade or tear either.

Sarsha, I had watched you for long enough and believed that someday you would receive the gown that was made just for you.

I am so glad that you have finally been able to trust me enough to take it and enjoy it as you do now.

Sarsha thanked him and was about to stand up and leave, when Manuel asked, would you mind if I had a look at the garments which you have with you in your basket.

But Manuel she cried as she sat down again, they are only rubbish compared to what you have given me, why would you bother wanting to see garments which I have made? I have never learnt how to make them as well as you do. Really, I have never been taught to make clothes at all.

I am still quite interested in seeing some of the styles which you have made Sarsha. You have given so many away, surely you have made many different kinds and surely they must have become better and better as you made more and more. Sarsha continued to relax further as she took some of the garments out of her basket to show Manuel, and found that as she did so she was able to comfortably smile at him.

I must admit, I have been trying to make them better and better as I made each one. I tried to do that especially when I was making it for someone that I felt perhaps had been through a really bad time and needed some kind of encouragement.

Oh Manuel, the eyes of those villagers are so sad most of the time. Perhaps the garments are keeping them a bit warmer than they were before. Manuel, some of the people have taken the garments which I have offered them, but I never see any of them wearing them as they continue to stand at their gateways each day, why do you think that is so?

You will understand some day Sarsha, but you must be patient until you see what is happening. Sarsha continued, I believe they must be grateful for what they receive, but they don't seem to be any happier. Manuel, sometimes my heart feels as though it will break into little pieces when I hear of their trouble and see their sadness. I just wish I could change things for them so as they don't have to suffer so much. Be patient and be careful Sarsha, they need to be ready in themselves before they can take any new action and begin to change the way of how they live.

Sarsha, if you like I can teach you how to make better garments, which will fit the people better. And sometimes if they are sewn together with special thread they will also last a lot longer. If you would like me to, we can start tomorrow.

Manuel, oh Manuel she cried I would like that very much indeed. I would like to learn the proper way of doing them but there is no way I can pay for any of the lessons. You see, I feel can barely afford the money for the thread to sew my garments. Sometimes I must buy the cheapest thread possible, just so I can keep going with the making of garments.

Does not worry about that said Manuel. My Father is rich beyond all your wildest imaginations. If you give your heart to this project and promise that you will do your very best to learn to sew for the villagers, then I know my father will give you all that you need to do it with. Sarsha, you also need to recognise that the money the money steward is minding for you is meant to buy the best of threads and supplies for your work for the villagers. This shocked Sarsha for she previously thought she still had to economise as much as possible to look like someone who managed her affairs well, or she may lose the supply of money.

Come here early tomorrow morning and we will go and see my father, then you can tell him all that you wish to do for the people of this village.

My father will also tell you how you can help make the villagers feel better about themselves and share some ideas with them of how to live a better and happier life without so much fear and sadness. But one thing at a time and lets attend to first things first.

Soon after the second goblet of that special hot milk had been drank, Sarsha stood up, thanked Manuel for all his kindness, promised to be there at sunrise and then left the strange little shop.

As she walked out the doorway, there again was the little boy and his puppy. This time they both stopped and the boy asked her where she got such a beautiful gown. You are so beautiful he said. Can I walk with you for a while I just want to look at your pretty gown? It seems to be changing colour all the time and yet it is always white. Then unexpectedly he scooped up the puppy and handed it to her. Here would you like to hold my puppy for a while?

As he placed the tiny puppy in her arms it began to lick her hand as she had seen it do to the boy many times. It began to bark with excitement. For a moment Sarsha was frightened that the puppy would tear her beautiful gown. But then as she held the puppy and saw how excited it was to be in her arms and felt how happy she was as she held something so warm and loving, she forgot all about her gown being damaged.

It wasn't long before they were at the castle gateway. Sarsha put the puppy down and he and the boy both ran off without another glance at her or her gown. She quietly went inside.

The following morning as the sun came up, Sarsha was happily getting ready to go and see Manuel. She wondered if she should take some more of the garments to give to the villagers on the way to Manuel's shop. As she looked in the large cupboards which had been filled with special materials for the garments, she saw that there were only a few scraps of material left and no threads at all to sew the garments together. Then she cried how can I possibly make any more garments for the villagers. And what has happened to all that beautiful material that was there when she first moved in to the castle. Then she attempted to count all the different garments she had made and given away. She lost count, she simply could not remember. She then realised that she had been concentrating for so long on getting the garments made and nothing else that she had lost sight of the fact that she had actually run out of material and threads. Then she remembered what Manuel had said about his father giving her all that she needed to make the garments for the villagers, if she was willing to learn well and work hard for them.

Sarsha could wait no longer. She closed her door and began to walk towards the little shop. Once again there was the little boy and his puppy. The boy was laughing and running all around Sarsha and the puppy. Sarsha bent down to pat the puppy as it ran between her feet tripping her over. At the same time the boy ran excitedly into her as well. So for a short time they all sat there in the middle of the dusty road just playing with each other. Sarsha had not laughed or enjoyed herself so much for a very long time. As she tried to stand up the little boy took her hand and helped her up. She was surprised at the strength that such a small hand had. He could only hold her hand but Sarsha could not deny the strength the boy had and it puzzled her. She started to brush down her dress to clean all the dust off what she thought would be on it and noticed how perfectly clean it was. Only then did she realise that she had unconsciously put on the same gown that Manuel had given her the day before.

Oh it is so beautiful she thought. I really do want to learn to make garments like this to give to others. It would be great if only I could help others to feel as clean and as beautiful as I do right at his moment.

Finally she set off again to Manuel's shop with the little boy and his puppy following close by all the way.

When she arrived at the shop, Manuel came out as he closed the door behind him.

Leons Castle

Manuel was happy to see Sarsha as well as the boy and his puppy.

Sarsha, do you see that big mountain just behind the shop, well that is where we are going now to see my father.

I honestly don't know whether or not I shall be able to climb it she said. Do not worry Manuel said I shall help you all the way up there.

It seemed to be a long time before they actually reached the bottom of the mountain where they could begin to climb up it.

As Sarsha and Manuel began to climb the mountain, the boy and his puppy ran off again, back towards the end of town where Sarshas castle was. Sarsha felt a little sadness as they left her so quickly but was excited at the same time about the journey she had began with Manuel.

Even though every part of this mountain was covered with spectacular scenery, truly beyond description, they did not stop for more than a few seconds as they came to each new place of majestic beauty.

For many years now, because of the problems to her legs Sarsha had been unable to do much walking for some time and now felt quite weak. She began to feel rather embarrassed not knowing how to ask Manuel if he could slow down and rest a while. She had begun to wonder in fact if she was going to survive until she got to the top, even though Manuel had told her he would help her all the way.

Suddenly, though it did not seem very long since they had started from the bottom of the mountain, yet here they were at a huge gateway of a castle larger than the mountains themselves which could be seen from every part of the street in the village below. Sarsha had never seen anything as big or as grand, so beyond all her abilities of description. She had never heard or read about anything of such magnitude. As she pondered these things she followed close behind Manuel every step of the way. Soon they had entered the door way of this unusual place and stood in what was like a foyer of a multi-storey mansion. There were large windows made of pure crystal with frames made of pure gold. All the walls were covered in the most exquisite tapestries she had seen, except one section which was off to the right of where she stood. The floors and the foot paths outside were made of highly polished marble with roses made of rare rubies inlaid evenly through them.

Sarsha was shocked because she knew that normally polished marble was quite slippery, but these floors were not so.

There was so much beauty surrounding her that Sarsha had forgotten for a short time that Manuel was still there with her. She certainly did not notice that Manuel's father had stepped up to her and had been speaking to her. Sarsha, Sarsha I would love for you to meet my father Leon.

Come inside Sarsha and sit by the fire for a while, you must be exhausted after such a long journey up the mountain. As she followed Manuel's father through to another large room, she suddenly realised that there were other people all around her, coming and going from all different directions. She was delighted to see how they all looked happy and healthy and talking so freely amongst themselves. She also noticed how their clothes seemed to be generally of the same type as the beautiful gown Manuel had given her. Then to her surprise she noticed as she looked closer their garments they were indeed exactly the same as hers.

With so much beauty and so many people all around her, Sarsha found that it was difficult to concentrate on what Manuel and his father had been saying. She seriously wondered how Manuel's father could take any time just to pay her any special attention when there were so many others that he could have been happier with.

Sarsha, Sarsha, would you like something to drink. Suddenly her attention was drawn back to Manuel and his father, and just as suddenly she felt as if she was the only one standing beside them.

To Sarsha, the beauty of the place was no longer noticeable as she began to listen more carefully to the words of Manuel's father.

He spoke softly and clearly and she heard him well and understood all that he had told her.

I am a stranger to him she thought, yet he is so willing to share many wonderful things with me. He is making me feel unusually special. For some strange reason he makes me feel as though I am personally special to him and just as important as Manuel his son is.

Manuel's father started to tell her of how Manuel had watched her so often with her lights on late of a night as she made the many garments for the villagers. That's strange she thought, has he too been watching me.

Sarsha became so preoccupied with her own thoughts that she had not noticed Manuel's father had come and stood right beside the chair where she now sat.

Sarsha, would you now like something to drink and perhaps something to eat as well? Only then did she realise how hungry and tired she really was. Oh yes please she whispered.

As he moved away to bring her something to eat and drink Manuel came to her side and began talking to her again. As he pointed out the specific picture in many of the different tapestries on the walls Sarsha was amazed at the beauty and the incredible colours which she knew she had never seen. It wasn't long before she could no longer handle just sitting there listening, she had to stand up and go and look for herself. The closer she came to them the more amazed she was with the quality of fine work in them.

Oh Manuel, these are so beautiful, where did they come from and who made them?

Manuel, the pictures are different to anything I have seen, how could anyone have imagined such beautiful things?

Sarsha my dear friend, these have come from many different countries. They are pictures of the memories many people have had about other people and wanted to tell my father about them.

They couldn't write the story or afford the materials to do paintings like famous artists. However in many villages across the lands for many years they have had wild cotton growing. They have learnt how to spin the thread from the cotton and dye it from the juice extracts from many different plants which grow in the forests and gardens that some people have been able to grow. But how did they get such a shine into some parts of it. Oh I see what you mean said Manuel. Well those parts are made form a fine thread they have extracted from a caterpillar called a silk worm. The process they have put it through has made it a shiny and high quality product to work with. Many of these tapestries are about memories of the beautiful things which have been done for the people. Some of these are from the village where you now live.

Come over here Sarsha, come and look at these here near the table where my father sits each night to eat his supper.

See this one here right near his chair, pay particular attention to the detail, the colour and the actual picture itself. She looked closely and stood there in silence for a long time.

Manuel came close to her again and gently touched her shoulder; Sarsha, what are you thinking about now, why are you so quiet?

She instantly began to cry. Oh it is so beautiful and yet somehow so sad. Who is that lady in the picture Manuel? Sarsha, don't you recognise her, or the garden or even the large door that she is sitting near?

It all looks a little bit familiar Manuel, but should I know her?

Sarsha have a closer look that is you. Do you remember that grubby looking lady that would not let you near her children so long ago; well she often used to sit just inside her door way in the dark, watching you as you sat alone. She noticed sometimes your tears would fall on some of the flowers at the edge of the foot path near you as you walked around your garden alone.

You know the purple and gold ones right near your front door way that have that strange and exotic perfume that fills your nostrils each time you walk inside your castle. Well dear Sarsha they are the ones in particular which your tears have been falling on for so long. It was the watering of your tears and the salt in them which gave such strength and abundant growth to them.

The old lady did not know how to talk to you, even after you gave her children those lovely warm clothed that you had made.

She could not afford to paint a picture, spin cotton or make colours from any plants. However she has a good friend that sometimes comes to see her from a far away village that is at the end of the road that goes past your castle. That friend of hers has spun much cotton and made many wonderful colours over the years. She wanted to show me the picture of the memory your neighbour has of you. Your neighbour has told her story to her friend many, many times. They have spent a lot of time together discussing how the picture was coming along and how it should be going. After a lengthy period of time they both agreed, this tapestry truly showed the best picture of what your neighbour thinks of you. The one who made it wanted me to know about it and take care of it because she felt that no one else was able to value it and take care in the way that it needed to be cared for.

I could not tell you about it earlier, because you would not have believed me. Besides that you had to come to my father's house to see all these other wonderful things as well, not just think or know about one small thing about yourself. Down in the village, in your castle or even in the gorge at the end of the road which goes past your castle, you would not have been able to see or take your time to appreciate these and many other things which I shall reveal to you each time you come here.

Just then Manuel's father came back into the room with a golden tray in his hands. On it were golden goblets of wine and several dishes of different kinds of meats and fruits.

Come he said, come and let us eat together, there is much I wish to share with you about making garments of great beauty and of lasting quality that fit perfectly and that will never wear out either.

It is now your perfect time to learn about these things and to gather the supplies that I will give you to make them. Then I will show you who you can give the garments to and in places that you haven't thought about before that are beyond the village below. But first let us eat and then rest for a while. Sarsha was quite surprised at how the meat seemed to melt in her mouth and the taste was something she had never imagined before let alone actually eaten. When she had finished eating the meat and dipping the small pieces of bread into the gravy eating that too with great delight, only then did she realise that there were figs and dates still left on the side of the plate. She turned to Manuel as she took one in her hand and began to put it into her mouth, I do love the taste of these but why are they with the meat on the same plate. I have eaten such fruits before but never with meat. Could you please explain why they are together like this, then she put the fig in her mouth.

Manuel smiled at her delight as she ate the fruit and also at the fact she was now comfortable enough to start asking questions that were important to her but without fearing what the angry response may have been. Sarsha, the meat was to give you strength for the rest of your time while you are here and the energy you will need to go back to your own castle at the other end of the street. But you see Sarsha, the fruit though they are nice to eat they also actually have some very important healing properties in them. You need that to have your body and your heart restored from the damage that has happened to them so often. Yes I know it happened so often that you gave up making any attempt to have something done for their healing. After you have received that special kind of healing you will become aware of other unusual strengths in you previously unrecognised to you. It will not be strengths you have been able to create for yourself, but it is what my father gives and helps you grow into. Why do I need something so different Manuel? Isn't it good enough for me to live the way I have been up till now. Yes it is good enough for what you have been able to do before, but now you are going to be doing many things in new ways and you of course need the appropriate new wisdom and strength. Because Sarsha, you are now from this moment onwards going to be often asked to do some, what may appear to be strange and unusual tasks for the villagers, for me and my father. As yet, the people of the village would not be able to directly receive our specific directions and special requests on their lives because so far they are still afraid to get to know us.

The Strange Room

Sarsha moved around a little as she attempted to stand up without knowing why.

Leon and Manuel smiled knowingly at each other. They delighted in watching this woman who was fully grown now acting as cheerfully and actively as a small child.

She stepped back a couple of steps from the table before she realised that Manuel and his Father were still seated.

Oh I am sorry perhaps I should have waited for both of you to leave the table first she laughed and was embarrassed at the strange sounds coming out of her mouth. No, definitely not Sarsha we were actually waiting for you and when you would be ready to take a walk around the rest of this room and enjoy a little bit of time with us before we gave you the new materials for the gowns you would be making back at your home.

Manuel, Manuel I have had a good look around this room and have seen all that is to be seen. With that comment she felt a little awkward and realised somehow she had judged the situation without knowing what Manuel was actually talking about.

I am sorry Manuel. But he only smiled at her as he walked to her side and took her by the hand while he turned her around to look off to the opposite wall of where they had all been seated.

If this is only one room Manuel, then why are those strange walls between that large wall over there and where we are standing? Again the strange sweet sounds fell from her mouth like crystal goblets gently tumbling against each other.

She was again shocked to think such sounds could come out of her. Again Manuel and Leon smiled knowingly at each other. Manuel took a few more steps towards the other wall and turned and squatted down on his haunches. Come on Sarsha; come on its time to go and investigate what it is that's all around you. Oh bother, why is he now talking to me like a baby she wondered? She felt awkward and realised she was leaning up against something which seemed to be right at her back and momentarily found she could not walk.

She turned her head and realised that Leon had quietly stepped right behind her in case she fell. She had unknowingly leant backwards and was now resting at the front of Leons huge legs. Suddenly she felt like a small child and looked down at her own legs and noticed that indeed they had become like a baby's legs. A little confused by now all she could do was listen to the sweet sound of Manuel in front of her calling gently to come forward. Leon moved slightly forwards and gave extra support to Sarshas legs which she needed to begin walking towards Manuel. She stumbled awkwardly then continued to move her little legs and found she was walking in a strange and quick way exactly as a baby would. By the time she reached Manuel she had returned to the normal size of the woman that she was before. She opened her mouth and began to laugh and cry at the same time. But the sounds quickly turned into singing and the same sounds of crystal goblets clanging together, she was singing now, no longer talking. Without thinking about it, with the last couple of steps towards Manuel, she actually jumped up into his arms and snuggled into his shoulder. Manuel held her tight till her laughing and crying had subsided.

Then gently put her down to stand on her own feet. I feel strangely stronger than I have before, and spun around like a small girl with her first fancy dress that she had ever owned. She was amazed at how far the edge of her gown had spread out as if there were many miles of sheer material draped from her waist. The colours were like rainbow crystals dancing all over her. Sparks like shards of crystal were flying all over the room, exploding like little stars. The edge of her gown was actually touching the walls all around her. By now Leon was standing beside Manuel, again they just quietly smiled at each other and waited for her to finish her time of excited celebration.

When she finished her dance of joy, Sarsha turned to look at where she had come from and realised with surprise they were no longer anywhere near the table where they had all sat at and eaten their meal.

Now Leon came close to Sarsha and asked her if she would like to see some of what was behind the first wall which was between them and the main wall at the other side. Yes please and again the same sweet sounds tumbled out of her mouth. She began to run around like an excited child not noticing where she was going and suddenly bumped into something that was soft yet unmoving. She stood still and looked to her side where she felt the bump and saw nothing more than a tall column of light that she could see straight through. She realised there was a whole line of this strange light and that in fact it was what she had previously thought to have been a strange yet solid wall.

As she moved around to see what this strange column nearest to her was really like, she noticed that the rest of the wall began to separate into many narrow columns. Each of them began to move like a vertical wave from top to bottom and back up to the top again. The light which began to spin and dance off from that wall was the same as that which shot off from her gown as she had danced. Leon came and took one of her hands as Manuel took the other and they began to dance with energy unknown to Sarsha. The wall continued to separate into columns and sounds like huge waterfalls began to tumble out in great abundance from the top of each column, as if voices of giants had began to sing.

Although the sounds were not really like words still Sarsha felt as though she was listening to a familiar song. As she, Manuel and Leon continued to dance and swirl around, they too began to have that same strange and wonderful sounds coming from their mouths. Sarsha began to weep with joy. She could not tell how long they had all been making sounds of delight and dancing around but suddenly had the desire to stop and just look around. Leon took both her hands and led her to another magnificent chair which was only inches away from the swaying wall. Come he said gently, come and sit a while. Though Manuel did not seem to leave the room and she couldn't tell where he had gotten it from, he handed her a lovely new goblet filled with strange, sweet drink which sparkled like liquid diamonds. I love you she blurted out spontaneously.

Then she was embarrassed at the thought of saying such words to a comparative stranger.

Leon understood exactly what she meant and attempted to calm her embarrassment by telling her that he and Manuel loved her as well and had indeed done so since the time she was born, but that they had to wait for the right time before they could tell her in specific words.

Now he said we can tell you many wonderful things without you being embarrassed or frightened of us.

Can we go and look at another one of those walls she asked as the first wall seemed to recede completely out of sight. First have a look at the floor and what else is really around you Sarsha.

Here have a look at this flower that seems to be hanging in mid air. What do you think is holding it there Sarsha? I don't have any idea she exclaimed as she went towards it to touch and smell it. One step towards it and the oil from its throat began to rise to the top of its petals. The rare, exotic perfume and the actual colour began to flow out and cover her. What am I supposed to do about this she cried, but still moved towards the flower? The purple colour from the inside of its petals seemed to wash over her and she felt as though the very substance of her gown was being changed by the touch of the colour. As Sarsha gently touched the edge of the flower she once again felt something gently touching her hand as she raised her eyes to ask the obvious question of what was that. She had caught a glimpse of colour and knew it was one of those columns of light which actually held the flower where it had appeared to be suspended in mid air. She then looked down and saw what appeared to be a cloud of purple mist moving around her legs, and they began to physically change. However this time they instantaneously grew taller than large trees. Feeling the strength in them gave her the feeling that they were like solid rock. She moved around to see how it felt to have such legs. In one move she leaped back to the other side of the room where the table was at which they had eaten. She opened her mouth again in delight, but this time with sounds of a mighty rushing river flowing out with sounds like that of a lions roar. Then again in one movement she leaped back to where she had been standing near Manuel and Leon.

Now they both said together, look down where you have just been leaping. She did and instantly saw that she had left foot prints behind. What are all these other foot prints, and really why did my feet leave such clear marks behind. That has never happened before. Oh yes it has Leon said, but you have never noticed it. All the other foot prints are those of the many people who have spent exactly the same kind of time here with us as you have, before they went back to their villages and separate places of work and dwelling.

Is it necessary for the prints to be so obvious Manuel? Yes they are for the tramping of the many soldiers of the world to follow and take direction from till they come here to stay. Sarsha was enthralled with the beauty of this room and gazed for many minutes at the continually moving walls of light. Soon she realised that she was not alone, there were many older folk, mostly men, silently walking to and fro appearing to talk. But she could not hear any sounds coming from their lips even though they were moving and forming words. Who are they Manuel? They are the old men and women from the village who had gone to war and never returned. No one can know where they are till the appointed time Sarsha or until they too have come here to stay.

Can I go and have a look at some more of these strange walls? No, not at this time but you can come to my supply room where I will show you and let you choose some materials for the making of the new gowns for the villagers and others

As she took in one simple breath, she was instantaneously in another room filled with white, pulsating light.

There before her was a small table covered in sheer material which was clear and colourless. Here Sarsha come and take as much as you want as I go and get the directions and patterns for you as to how I want you to do them in future. Leon was back within moments and gave her one pattern and a sheet of paper with two words on it. That is not clear directions she commented and there is only one pattern. How am I to ever cut the right size, shape and the right style for all the different sizes of the villagers and the unknown others. How come there is only a small table filled with this material cant I choose from all the rest as well. No you are not ready yet for that and besides there are special elements to the material which makes it unnecessary to have any other different ones. You will find out about that later.

All the material on this table is clear of colour but as you follow the steps and pattern which I have given you, you will see that each garment will have its own colour developing as you complete the sewing of it. Now please Sarsha have a look at the directions I have given you. There were only two words on it. She turned the paper over and over looking for the rest of the directions. She was looking for the familiar things she could have worked with and control as she had done over the last long period of time as she sewed all the other garments. Well Sarsha, what do you see? Just two words Manuel, where are the rest of the directions, why can't it be a lot clearer than this? Read the words out loud Sarsha. Trust me. Then she knew she would be alright somehow as she just kept on working on the garments.

You will be fine Sarsha said Leon, just think of this day each time you are making something and are looking for more accurate direction, trust me and you will know what to do.

Now it is time for you to go back to your castle for a while. But I want to stay here much longer she pleaded. You can come back any time you want to, but for now you need to share what little you have seen here. The day will come Sarsha that you will be able to stay here forever but you are not ready for that just yet, and besides there is much for you to do in the village first. Can I look at least one more of those strange walls. Next time you come here you can but not now.

She reluctantly gathered the material together which she had decided to take, put them in a basket which she noticed was weightless, and began to walk to where she thought the door way to the room was. Before she knew it she was walking down the first level of the road going out from the castle doorway.

She looked around and could no longer see Leon but Manuel was still beside her as she continued to walk silently down the mountain.

Soon they came to what appeared to be a gate way which strangely stood by itself but there were no other landmarks or fences bordering off any particular part of the property. The gate way was ancient and just inside it was a golden grape vine which towered above them appearing to touch the sky itself. At first Sarsha did not recognise it as a vine until Manuel told her to go closer and have a better look. She saw clearly that it was quite old and felt it was also dead. How was it ever possible for a vine made of gold to actually grow any grapes she asked. One day you will understand the answer to that Sarsha and you won't have to ask for it again either. How long has it been there she enquired? From the beginning of time he responded. Why is the beginning of the actual branches so high up from the ground? If grapes ever grow on it no one will be able to pick them. Do not worry Sarsha, the day will come and you will see exactly who picks the grapes. The branches are so high up because for a long time when the grapes were growing lower on the vine, wild creatures would come and destroy them as they travelled through attempting to climb this mountain. Will I have to come through this gate way each time I come to this mountain Manuel. Oh yes you will, because even though you do not see any fence there, you will never be able to enter through the invisible yet unbreakable boundaries of this mountain.

She checked her legs to see if they were still as huge as they had been for a time in that wonderful room. But no, they were now back to normal again and she had begun to feel some of the pain which she had known over the last many years. It's alright Sarsha Manuel said in response to her thoughts. You may feel your legs are not strong enough to do all you will be asked to, but trust me you are going to do well with all that I ask of you because I know exactly how much you can or cannot do.

As they continued through the gateway and down the mountain, Sarsha noticed something glistening on the ground which ran at each side of the road in front of her. She stopped and bent down to look closer and saw that it was a type of golden oil. It continued the whole way down to the end of the street where Manuel's shop was. There they said a brief good bye and Sarsha expressed her desire to return again and often, if she was allowed. Oh yes you can certainly go up the mountain any time you want now that I have taken you for the first time. You can go as often as you want but I would sometimes like to go with you as well if you are comfortable with that.

As Sarsha continued down the mountain and towards her castle deep in thought about the many wonderful things she had just experienced on the mountain, her memories were drawn to the many wonderful sights and things which covered the mountain. Sweeping smaller mountain ranges, valleys filled with laughter and the sounds of strange sweet music, trees that had the largest and brightest fruit covering them, exotic flowers which were brighter, bigger and sweeter than she had seen, forests filled with strange tall trees which gave off a powerful smell of freshness. The trees swayed backwards and forwards with small creatures moving so fast Sarsha couldn't see what they were. The forests swelled with the sounds of many different birds and the sounds of the multitude of those animals which she could not see. There were sweeping hills and shallow valleys covered with different green grasses in the front area of the castle many different varieties of short fruit trees heavily laden with fruit, and patches of strange flowers on both sides of her. The flowers were in scattered clumps like treasures dropped accidently on the ground and left behind carelessly. Sarsha wondered at their bright and variegated colours which were surprising her with each glimpse of their beauty, size and shape as she walked on. Is there no end to the diversity of life here on this great mountain she mused? Will I ever see all of it? Why didn't I see any of this before she wondered? And what about those many tall buildings of which I haven't noticed before? I wonder who it is that lives in them or are they just abandoned like my castle was for so long in the village?

Suddenly there was one of those magnificent columns of light which she saw in the great room on the mountain, beside her, which still didn't appear to have any specific form of a human, and it simply said Sarsha, the day will come when you will have perfect and full freedom to walk through these hills and see up close all that you have had a brief glimpse of this morning. You will get to meet many of the people who live in those mansions and you will eat bountifully and as often as you want of all the fruit and other foods on this mountain. Just be patient, your time will come. Then the column vanished as quickly as it had appeared. She continued down the street beyond the place where Manuel had his weavers shop. But still deep in thought she did not hear many of the villagers calling out and waving to her as she walked past them. As she stepped into the gate way of her own castle horse whinnied at her, and she stopped briefly to pat him and whisper a few soft words of greeting. As she continued towards her door way she noticed the glistening oil had not entered into her gate way but indeed had continued on and passed by towards the end of the street. She determined to investigate where the running oil ended up, but that would have to wait for a while because she first wanted to get busy with the making of the new clothes to see how well the colours would be forming as she sewed.

As Sarsha put the large key into the lock she smelt a strange yet somehow familiar perfume and looked all around her to try and find it. She then saw on the ground near her feet a purple flower growing straight out of the ground but not on any plant or bush, similar to the one she had seen in the room of the castle on the mountain. Its perfume too was warm and strong and wrapped all around her as she entered her door way.

She walked towards the small room where she always sat to do her sewing. As she looked around in there she saw the last few remnants of cloth which remained after all the garments she had made in the past. What she originally thought was the most beautiful material, now faded in comparison to the material she had brought down from the mountain.

She lit her fire and sat close by it, staring at what she held in her hands unable to physically continue because of her desire to excel in any future garments she would be making. The room was soon filled with the soft glow of the fire and with the perfume which still clung to her legs which had wrapped itself around her as she entered her front door, but it was strangely now growing stronger and stronger all the time. It was as if someone had distilled the oil of many of the same kind of the flowers and placed it in a bowl and was now walking towards her with it.

She felt the gentle touch of something softly brushing her face and turned to see what had done it and there right by her side was one of the same columns of light which had come from the wall in the castle. She remembered how the wall had seemed to divide over and over into multiple tall columns of beautiful light. Now the column spoke and asked her what she really wanted to do with the material which she was still holding.

I want to get on with making the clothes which Leon and I had discussed but I am now afraid again of not doing a good enough job of it. Don't you remember what he had said about the directions of the two words which were written on the paper Sarsha? Yes, but how do I begin to design the pattern and what size and so forth shall I begin with. Oh come on Sarsha deep down you know you can do it. But you doubt only because the way of it is so different to any previous knowledge you've had of what you can do or control. Sarsha you are so sceptical about it all. Just put the material on the table and begin to cut it and I promise you it will all go well. Sarsha did as she had been directed and then remembered the two words on the paper {Trust Me} She began to cut and was amazed to see and feel the flow and direction of the materials as it took on the shape of a gown.

Soon she had cut and prepared to make a fully grown woman's gown in a style she had never known before.

The column of light began to move around the room like sparkling stream of water suspended in mid air. The sweetest music began to flow from the edges of it and filled the room and Sarsha mind. She began the hand sewing of the gown and lost all concentration of time. As she finished the last stitch and put the sewing on the table she noticed that the beautiful music, light and perfume ceased to be. She had sewn throughout the night again and not realised it. She stood up and stretched her legs and felt a strength in them which surprised her. She heard horse whinnying and acting unusually excited about something or other. She went to the door to see what was happening, and saw to her great surprise some of the village women at the gate way.

What is wrong she proclaimed? Why are you are all here at this time of the day and in fact why are you here at all? Still unknown to Sarsha personally, the old woman who had told the story for the making of the beautiful tapestry which was hanging in the castle on the mountain began to speak. I heard the strange music coming from your place last night and because I had never heard it before I wanted to investigate what it was. I called for these other women to come with me because I was frightened to come alone. They too have never heard such strange yet beautiful sounds, so we stayed here all night at your gate way listening to it. The darkness between your gate way and your door way seemed too far for us to go through. We did not know what may have been hiding there waiting to harm us if we dared to go through and we were afraid of that too.

Then when we saw those strange flashes of light darting to and fro inside your place we wondered for a while if you were alright, because we thought perhaps your place was on fire. So then, are you alright? Sarsha was shocked at this genuine enquiry in regards to her well being and she openly wept. The old lady then actually entered the gate way and put her arms around Sarsha, while the other ladies held back. I am so tired Sarsha wept, but would love you to come in and have a cup of tea with me and talk a while before I go to bed. Can I bring the others too the old lady enquired? Oh yes, yes definitely and she turned and beckoned for the others to follow, which they did without any further hesitation.

After Sarsha made a quick cup of tea for them all she asked them to follow her into the special room where all her sewing had been done of the past times. They were amazed at the beauty and vast variety of what met them there. Sarsha picked up the gown she finished only moments before. Here, would you like to have a look at it as she handed it to the old lady. As the woman took the gown in her hands the colour of it began to dance and change with every movement. The woman was frightened and dropped it. Sarsha picked it up and handed it back to her. I have never held anything so beautiful; it feels strangely light and smooth. Then she wondered silently to herself what it would look like on her but wasn't game to think of owning anything so beautiful. Just for my own curiosity Sarsha asked, why don't you go and try it on in the small room over behind that curtain near the wall. I haven't made one without a pattern before so I have no idea how it will look on anyone or how it has turned out. Surprisingly the old lady was no longer afraid and agreed to try it on. When she stepped out again from behind the curtain she appeared to be floating on air. Her height was greater; her face was shining as was her hair and she appeared to be many years younger as she smiled at Sarsha. It was obvious to all that the gown fitted perfectly as if it was specially designed and sewn just for her. How did you know what size to make she asked excitedly? I didn't I just had to trust what Leon had told me up on the mountain. Who is this Leon asked the old lady? He is the father of Manuel. Who then is Manuel?

He is the man who works and lives at the other end of the village street in that strange little shop which no one wants to go and have a look in. I shall take you there one day if you like. You will truly be surprised at how good it is to enter such a small place. Do you want to come with me next time I visit him. Oh yes please. The other women standing nearby did not want to miss out. They were excited with what was happening and at the prospect of them too seeing what Sarsha had seen and experienced. Sarsha knew deep in her heart that the gown belonged to the one who was now wearing it.

I truly want you to keep that gown, it is yours she said.

The old lady broke down and cried for a long time as Sarsha held her gently in her arms. I want to keep it but feel so unworthy of such a garment. Sarsha remembered only too well what it had felt like in the past when she wore old rags for so long, then what it felt like when she tried the first gown on which had been in those large cupboards. Then the overwhelming sweet sadness as she put on the gown which Manuel had made and given her that day long ago. She smiled to herself for she knew well that the old lady was now headed in the direction of making many changes as she took the necessary steps towards receiving her very own garment from Manuel. Sarsha sensed a growing peace in the old lady as she held her and believed that she was probably going through some healing of deep memories which she had never shared with another soul. The old lady opened her mouth to speak and the same kind of sweet tinkling fell from her mouth as it had with Sarsha some time earlier, as she too had attempted to form words.

Sarsha then turned to the other women as they looked on and softly asked them if they too would like a gown made for them. I still have a large amount of material left and it is only for making garments for the people of this village. They were shocked but still happy enough to say yes please.

Be patient and I will make them as soon as I possibly can Sarsha explained as the women left chattering excitedly amongst themselves. The old woman began to twirl around like a young girl as she danced her way back down the street towards her home.

Not long afterwards, Sarsha did take that whole group of women to meet Manuel. Then at a later day took them up the mountain to meet Leon. After that she left them to decide for themselves what they wanted to do about further visits to the small shop and to the mountain top.

Sarsha enjoyed the company of the women more as the days continued, but she enjoyed many hours and indeed many days on her own and in fact preferred to visit Manuel and Leon on her own. Over the next many days Sarsha was either returning to the mountain or spending many hours sewing more of the gowns made from the beautiful material. Or she would be simply sitting and chatting to Manuel as he also continued to make the many gowns he knew he would be passing on to many of the villagers and others which would be coming to the shop in years to come. She sat for hours at a time silently watching as Manuel would be spinning the cotton and the fine, shiny silk and then weaving them into the amazing material needed for the gowns. Each time she went to the mountain Leon would talk with her, sharing many wonderful and new things of how there was a higher, more pure form of knowledge to learn on the mountain top. She would come to see in time what joyful and unusual things there were to do and enjoy for the people who were permanently living there. Each time they would go close to another of the walls which had been there from the very first time she visited. Each wall was directly and uniformly arranged in staggered heights from the front to the back row. Although it appeared that each layer of the walls were actually connected to each other, creating one solid form there was always a greater world of beauty, people, strange creatures, and more beautiful music than behind the previous one. The multitude of voices was now becoming clearer and clearer with the passing through of each wall. Between some of the walls the further towards the back as they went through each one, it became evident that the multitude of people was ever increasing and moving around busily yet calmly attending to whatever was in front of them to be done. Sarsha could not make herself heard to those people but Leon had encouraged her to know that one day she would be able to do so. She wondered a great deal who they were and why they were there. She noticed that they all were strong of frame, tall and unusually beautiful. They moved around in constant joy ever willing to help others even though they may have had things of importance to attend to for themselves. After some time she heard what they were saying but mostly the words were of a foreign language. The few words she could understand clearly were still strange to her because she had never heard words being used in that context before about people, places and things previously unknown to her.

Each of those luminous walls, as all previous ones had done, divided into many luminous, tall columns of strange flashing, sparkling lights and music, swaying backwards and forwards as if in time to some perfect tune heard and known only to them. Each time that she approached the walls and the columns as they were dividing off from the original solid form, they were continually taking on minute details similar to a male human form.

Number One Wall

She noticed that behind the first wall they were mostly mature age men and a few mature age women. Who are these folk? Sarsha remembered asking Leon. Well they are the men from the village who had gone off to war or to find food and supplies for their families and never returned. They came here when they could no longer go on or were able to return to the village because they had no further strength left in them. One by one with each return visit to see Leon they continued to approach the next wall. Each time the wall divided off into those identical, magnificent columns of light.

Behind the second wall there were many of Sarshas relatives and other folk which she had known throughout her life. She knew some of them had died but many of them she had no contact with and had only heard her family speak of as distant relatives. One woman in particular which had walked past Leon and Sarsha as if she didn't see them seemed familiar to her. Who is she wondered why does she seem to look a lot like me? Sarsha, Leon responded to her thought that is your great grandmother which you never met. She was actually the last one to have taken care of the castle you now live as you care for the village people. She also had the same ability to make clothing as you do and to tell stories to the village children.

The gown you had on the first day you went to Manuel's shop was actually the last one she had made.

Behind the third wall were large numbers of small children, some in fact being carried around by beautiful luminous beings which appeared to be the same as the sections of walls of light.

Who are they Leon she had asked. Sarsha my dear, many of them are the babies which were still born in the village. Some of them are the children which had died in that terrible cave which you had gone in and out of to try and encourage them to come out of. The stench you smelt each time you entered the mouth cave was of the bodies of many dead ones, as they lay there unknown to the outside world. You never knew they were there so you could have never brought any of them out. No one else knew where they were either and therefore never knew where to look for them even though their hearts ached to find their lost children and have them at home again in their arms.

Sarshas heart ached at this news and her legs lost all strength, she could no longer stand and fell to the floor. But she was surprised when one of the tiny ones slowly walked towards her and gently touched her on the face. Come on mummy, come on its alright I am not hurting anymore, I am safe and I am really happy. Come on mummy come and play with me for a little while before you go home again. Leon moved silently to Sarsha side and helped her to rise to her feet then stepped back a few steps from her. Come on mummy and I will show you something beautiful where I often go to play and run around. Without stopping to think Sarsha picked up the little boy and hugged him till he started to wriggle and hop down. Come on mummy and he grabbed her hand and they ran like deer swiftly off to the special place he had spoken of. It only seemed to be a few seconds but they were soon at the edge of a shallow stream surrounded by lush grass and many different kinds of sweetly perfumed flowers. They both sat in the soft, warm grass holding each other's hand. Look mummy at the sparkles in the water, can you see how the fish are blowing bubbles in the air. Now look here mummy and he tugged her hand to turn her around. There were hundreds of many different coloured butterflies skipping across the bubbles as each of them rose into the air. Sarsha was captivated by the colour of one of them in particular, which was a brilliant, iridescent blue as it came close and sat momentarily on the boy's nose.

A few other tiny children came close and attempted to catch some of the butterflies as they giggled and ran around without a care to slow them down or to hold them down in any way.

Sarsha began to cry without understanding why. Mummy, mummy stop crying you don't have to worry any more. Sarsha was enjoying the company and the touch of the little boy but was a little frightened because of her uncertainty about her strange emotions and what was happening. Why do you keep on calling me mummy, who are you and what is your name she cried. Mummy, my name is John don't you remember when I left you before it was time for me to go into the world.

I am happy here but I can still remember how you carried me inside you for those few short months a long time ago. I know you have missed me but I really am happy and having lots of fun here. I never have to worry about there being enough light for me to play in and see where I am going. Mummy it was very dark inside you and I couldn't see where all the noise was coming from outside you. I am sorry, but I couldn't wait to go and play and so Leon told me I could come here and be with Him forever and ever.

Mummy can you please go and tell the other mummies and daddies that their babies are O.K. now, so they don't have to keep on crying and hurting. Tell them they too can go and sit by the water and watch the bubbles that the fish blow out and watch the butterflies as they dance on top of the bubbles. Sarsha had no words left to speak but swept up little John into her arms and held him so close she could hear and feel his heart beat on top of her own.

Mummy I have to go to bed now and you must go home for a while but can you first walk with me back into that special room for a little while. I want to show you something else. They were soon back in the room again where Leon stood waiting with the strangest and sweetest smile which gave strength and deep encouragement to her aching heart. Come on mummy just over here near the next wall. She followed silently and suddenly all the tiny ones in the room began to run towards the next wall. Some of them were floating through the air on wings of pure light.

The whole room filled with the sounds of laughter and sweet singing as the ones who flew went to the top of what now appeared to be more like a sheer white, crystal, and gauze curtain. Although it was sheer nothing could be seen through it until the little ones that were flying went to the top of it and all the other little ones gathered closely at the bottom. Suddenly the columns of light which had divided off from all the solid formation began to sing one note which continued unceasingly. Sarsha noticed how all of the other columns which had been dividing off gathered together now at this one place. Many different harmonies of sweet yet powerful music spontaneously filled the dips and hollows of light as they danced all around. Then all the little ones assisted by the many columns of light pulled together and the curtain ripped from top to bottom and they all stood at the entrance of the great hall of the palace. At the front section of the hall was a huge throne where a silent extremely tall king, dressed in exquisite gowns sat watching all the proceedings around him. That man is familiar to me Leon Sarsha bubbled as she turned to speak to him. But he was no longer there. She turned again and realised it was indeed Leon that sat upon the throne robed in glorious, regal gowns. He appeared to be as tall as many houses on top of each other. The throne was surrounded by more of those tall columns of light swaying and dancing as they sang over and over, Oh mighty king all this glory and power is yours. Come over here for a little while Sarsha and sit with me. She did so in total silence as the music and the marvellous light continued their great display of celebration. She sat there silently for a short while until Leon whispered to her, you need to go home to your own castle Sarsha you have things to do there still. Little john ran up to her and took her by the hand again as he led her to the entrance of the castle, where he hugged her leg tightly and said, see you again soon mummy, but I must go to bed now, bye, bye and he was gone.

Sarsha began her journey home again and found there was plenty of light to see where she was walking even though it was now night time in the village below. I feel so tired she thought but this time she felt no pain in her legs as she began walking back towards her gate way at her palace.

She felt safe enough even though it was night time and her memories drifted continuously back to the wonderful things which surrounded her on the mountain top. Without thinking about it she had walked down the opposite side of the street to where all the houses were. It was strangely dark there with the appearance of tall black bushes and hills. There was nothing that ever drew her attention to this side of the street. In fact she hardly gave it a second thought at any time. She occasionally gave a brief glance down at the cobblestones which made up what she previously thought was only the edge of the road. Again she noticed something glistening in the moon light. She bent lower as she continued walking and saw golden oil still flowing down the road in the direction which went past her castle. She had lost concentration and suddenly tripped on one of the stones and fell breaking her right leg in three places. In anger and fear she began spitting out harsh and sometimes crude words. Sarsha was blaming the stupid person who may have put such rotten rocks in her way forcing her to hurt herself. She knew it was an irrational outburst but for several minutes could not stop herself and the anger which seemed to be growing in her heart.

Can I help you Sarsha Manuel softly asked? No you can't, just go away and get out of my way I can do this on my own she spluttered as she attempted to stand, instantly falling flat on her back. Are you sure I cannot give you a helping hand Sarsha I really don't mind. Oh shut up Manuel she spat out, why are you being so nice to me anyway? He did not give up on her and offered again. This time Sarsha realised she was being totally rude to one who had given so much care and attention to her for so long. I must have really hurt him she thought and cried with the great shame she felt for herself. I just wanted to manage by myself she thought and here is this gentleman trying to help me, but instead is making me feel like a totally useless fool. Why can't I just be strong enough to do everything by myself without having to depend on others to help me while I looked weak in front of others?

I would really like to help you Manuel persisted gently as he stooped down and gathered her up in his arms. Sarsha began to weep uncontrollably. No one has ever picked me up from the ground whenever I have fallen and hurt myself before and I thought I was too heavy and too bad for them to bother trying. How come you are able to do so, especially after the way I have treated you Manuel. My love for you is making me stronger than others who simply didn't know how to pick you up Sarsha. But from now on that will be very different for you.

As Manuel began to walk away from the side of the road and down towards Sarshas castle she heard a great ripping sound as if material was being torn. Oh dear what was that she asked. Look there by the road side Manuel said. Sarsha sank further into the warmth and safety of Manuel's arms as she saw what appeared to be black cloth being torn apart and burning at the same time while pieces of it disintegrated and floated away.

That deep darkness which has seemed to be like bushes and hills at the road side has been developed over many centuries. It has been formed by the anger, the pain, the fear, the doubt and the unforgivenes of the people of the village, you included. Every time they were hurting or afraid or getting to the point of mistrusting all mankind they would try to throw off what was really happening instead of facing it and trying to deal with it. Sarsha, Because the fear, anger, unforgiveness and the pain of their lost loved ones has gone on for so long it has created an atmosphere of all that has built up into a strong wall of darkness. The darkness has blinded them emotionally and mentally and has stopped them from going out beyond the limits of the village. It has been such a strong wall that many people from outside of the village have not been able to enter with all the goods and supply's needed in the village and for its people.

When you accepted my help tonight and finally allowed me to lift you up I was able simply with my breath, to break down the wall and its ability to block out light and life. I am helping you now but many others are going to be able to become interested in the new opening into the village also. I am so sorry Manuel for such bad behaviour towards you. I really do understand Sarsha but I will also be helping you to be less fearful and to talk the way you desire with strong but good words towards me and all others. I see you as someone quite special and in time you will learn to see and appreciate yourself the same way. As all that begins to happen you will then be more interested in helping the women of the village to find their peace and joy again and not quite as interested in just making beautiful gowns. Sarsha dear, keep on inviting some of the women in to have a drink and a talk and you shall soon see how things in the village and its people begin to openly change. Soon they were at the gate of her castle and as Manuel stood there carefully holding her; she could clearly hear the whinnying of horse. Again she noticed there was something glistening near Manuel's feet, but still only running past her gateway and not into it. I must investigate that tomorrow she thought, I really do have to find out what it is about. I will not be putting it off any longer. I think you shall have to wait a while before you do that Sarsha, Manuel softly whispered.

She put her hand on the gate to open it and a flash of bright blue light filled the sky off to her left then hovered momentarily over the top of her and Manuel. Still holding the gate she turned to look and saw that the vibrant light was dancing and filling the whole sky. She noticed that it was the same colour as the butterfly which had momentarily sat on little Johns nose. This is all so beautiful she thought as Manuel carried her inside and sat with her on the throne in the great hall of her castle with her still cradled in his arms like a baby.

Manuel I am frightened with the way I spoke to you when you first offered to pick me up. Why Sarsha? Well to begin with, you were only offering to help me and I was clearly nasty to you, what if I do that again are you just going to stop caring for me and leave me where I am next time? And what if some day I get angry enough to really harm someone with my words or even strike out physically and hit them. No Sarsha I shall never give up on you, but I will only pick you up or help you if you let me. I was there watching all the other times when you displayed such anger and spoke with words like a snake spitting venom. But you see dear Sarsha, I knew all those bad things that those men did and other people when they thought they had the right to do as they pleased.

I knew how afraid you were to tell anyone about it. I watched as you cried yourself to sleep night after night and that was before you went into that cave thinking you would be finally safe. You went in there thinking that the pain and the memories would all go away. But how do you feel now Sarsha? Do you think you have forgiven them yet? Oh yes for sure she responded too quickly. Then why Dear Sarsha did you fearfully explode like you did towards me at the side of the road where you fell?

Manuel, deep inside me I feel there is always the possibility of the same things happening and still that I would not be able to tell anyone about it and get some help. So really why should I forgive them at all, why should I forgive such thing regardless to who does them she cried? Firstly Sarsha, forgiving them does not say they are right it does however release you from the tightness in your heart and you shall be able then to move around and sleep better of a night time. I have never thought of that she responded. O.K. then I do forgive them but it does not seem fair to me in any way.

Also Sarsha you do not know what those people have been through to have made them act towards you the way they did. The day may come when they too will let someone help them, then they shall be able to stop being so angry and hurtful to others. But for Now Sarsha just let it all go and rest for a little while before you try to work out the problems of everyone else. As she continued to listen to the calmness and yet strength of Manuel's words her heart began to settle into a peaceful flow of strangely different thoughts. Now she had a deep sense of joy and peace which was filling her whole being. Her heart felt strangely light and her shoulders which had been bent and weak for as long as she could remember were now straight and relaxed. Sasha tried to ponder all the wonderful things she had seen and heard but it was too much for her and soon fell into a deep and restful sleep. Manuel put her to bed, lights the fire and then quietly leaves the castle. It took many months before she was well enough to walk again.

The night after Manuel carried Sarsha to her castle he came back with the old lady who had passed on the story for the tapestry. Sarsha was surprised at the unannounced entry but still pleased to see them for she knew it would be some time before she could do anything for herself. Manuel stood beside her bed while the woman left the room after a short greeting and soon came back with a meal beautifully set out on a tray and one single deep purple flower. Isn't that the flower that was at my door way she asked? Oh yes it certainly is Sarsha, but wait till you see what has happened along your path way when you are able to walk out there and have a look.

What is your name Sarsha asked? She had shared some conversation and a few cups of tea with her but never thought to ask her name before this. Lenora, the woman replied.

What is that strange light outside asked Sarsha? I can see it even though my curtains are still closed.

Manuel then stepped closer and gently held her hand as he sat on the side of her bed. Sarsha, after I brought you home last night there was a mighty storm of which this village has not seen the like of before. The winds howled and the torrential rain poured down all night. Now the cobble stones along the side of the road can be seen, where you had previously thought was nothing more than a wall of black rocks and dead black bushes. It is quite bright and shiny. The rain has washed away all the dark soil and revealed the golden beauty of them and the rocks are obviously reflecting the glittering light all through the village.

What do you mean golden beauty Manuel she asked? That strip of roadside was actually the rocks of gold which the workers placed there among the other blue metal rocks when the road was originally built. This village has been well known for the many huge deposits of gold and the builders wanted all visitors to know of the hard work it took to construct all the buildings and roadways here. They wanted visitors to enjoy their beauty as well as their usefulness. Manuel then left as Lenora and Sarsha happily talked on.

I shall get rather bored if I have to sit here and do nothing for any length of time Lenora. I don't feel I can sew any of the gowns which I have been doing while sitting in bed, because I cannot even cut them out. Is there some way I can help you Sarsha? Sarsha felt that she had to be honest with herself at that point but could not speak her words of serious doubt to Lenora about her having any sewing skills whatsoever. She asked Lenora if she could bring some of the material in the basket which was in the room next door.

Lenora did so and came back with a smile right across her face. What has suddenly made you so happy Sarsha asked?

Sarsha, when I entered that room I saw many things which I remember hearing about when I was a small girl. My mother had spoken many times of the crafts and things her grandmother used to do when she was a little girl. Well, when I entered that room next door I saw some of what had been described to me so long ago.

I shall have to have a closer look next time I am in there Sarsha responded as she continued to wonder how to handle the present situation.

She decided to ask anyway, Lenora have you ever sewn this type of material? No was the response, but I would love to have a try. Between them they decided to bring in the table from the next room so Sarsha could watch on as she talked Lenora through the process.

However from the moment Lenora began to lay out the material on the table and started cutting it, Sarsha was embarrassed to see that she was indeed a much more proficient worker than could have been imagined.

Within just one a day Lenora had cut out and completely sewn up a magnificent gown as she chatted to Sarsha. In between her hours of work, she had also cooked Sarsha meals and helped her to bathe.

Sarsha was definitely reminded of her loss of self sufficiency. When night time fell Sarsha was quite tired and just longed to sleep with no one else around. Again she felt awkward about asking Lenora to do anything let alone ask her to go home. Aren't you tired she asked her and don't you want to go to bed by now?

I would love to Sarsha but my house and many others were totally destroyed last night during the storm. I thought perhaps I could just work here all night. Oh dear me no Lenora that is not right. Why don't you stay in the room the other side of the sewing room and we shall talk about it again in the morning. When morning cam Lenora came early again with Sarshas breakfast beautifully set out on the golden tray and there was yet another purple flower in a small crystal vase, but this time there was also one golden flower with it. This time Sarsha didn't need to ask about the golden flower, for she now remembered seeing some small gold flowers right along both sides of her foot path from the gate way to the palace door. She had not however taken very much notice of them.

This was the general procedure for the next many days. On some occasions Lenora would invite a couple of the other ladies from the village to come and have a chat to Sarsha, which they did so quite willingly. Most nights they would not leave till dark. Sarsha then asked them after they did this for two or three nights in a row why they left so late. Sarsha we have no homes left since the night of the storm and we have been sleeping on the side of the road since that time.

Then what have you been eating since then she asked. Since the time of the deep darkness and the coldness that it brought, someone has been leaving food at our door way every night. We don't know who has been doing it, and to be honest we don't eat some of what they leave there because we don't know what it is. We have been throwing it out the back of where our homes used to be our place. Whoever it was leaving the food they were also leaving some strange looking stones. All of the villagers have been throwing the stones and most of the food out the back of their place because we simply don't know what they are or how to use them. This sparked a deep curiosity in Sarsha and a determination to find out one day what the stones were. She thought about asking Manuel, Leon or perhaps even the money steward about it. She asked the two women their name. One was Bekany the other Sapphira. Why don't you go and see if you would be comfortable in the same room with Lenora where she is staying, if so you can stay there till something else can be arranged.

They went to look and came back bubbling with excitement. After being asked about their obvious joy, they explained how they had been drawing back the curtains in Lenora's room and discovered a passage way which led off to many other rooms. Sarsha commented to the fact that she had never been in that room and had no idea what was hidden there. The three women then went and investigated further, with greater care and found that there was indeed a whole section of rooms not seen from the outside of the castle and certainly not within range of sight from Sarshas room. They explained in great detail that there were many other rooms fully furnished, a smaller hall a kitchen, bathroom, toilet and an unusually large laundry room.

From what they described Sarsha recognised that it was probably the servant's quarters from the time of her grandmother being the queen there in residence. Lenora, Beckanny and Sapphira you may as well go and live in there. I shall never use those quarters. You don't have to pay any levy or rent, but if you could just help me from time to time with some of the work that Leon and Manuel ask me to do that would be very much appreciated. They were delighted with the offer and instantly accepted. But they all three explained to her that they had actually been waiting to help her with whatever she was making for so many nights in a row as they watched her sitting with only candle light hour after hour. They never asked her about it because they were afraid she would reject their offer because she felt there wasn't any value in the work of a poor villager.

With the assistance of the three women early the next morning Sarsha went down to the money keeper and arranged for an extra withdrawal of money for all the necessary food and cleaning supplies she now needed for the extra women.

When all the women arrived back at the palace Sarsha sat in the back garden while the other three set about to make some lunch. She had drifted off to a light sleep as the songs of the many little birds sang in the tree tops. Horse whinnied from time to time but the sounds of it seemed to be far away and didn't disturb her rest at all.

Lenora came rushing excitedly out to her, awakening her with a startle. Sarsha there is someone here to see you. As Lenora came fully to the front of where Sarsha sat another woman followed close behind. She was of medium build and looked powerful in the way she walked, yet when she spoke it was like a breeze over a bubbling brook.

After a brief introduction she sat near Sarsha on the wooden bench seat. Some small talk was shared about the weather and bright sunshine. Then the woman introduced herself, hello I am Natasha. I am the lady that has been visiting Lenora for many years. I am also the woman who made the tapestry which depicts what she had felt and seen about you, even though she was unable to speak to you personally at the time and tell you for herself.

I live in the country which is in the direction at the end of the road which passes you castle. What is your country like Sarsha asked? It is greatly different to this country, it is much hotter. There are many jungles and rain forests where tropical flowers and many kinds of unusual animals live. One of our main features besides our beautiful flowers is the many varieties of butterflies. Sarsha loved the description she was receiving from Natasha but found it impossible to accept it as a real place that actually existed, and seemingly so close to where she lived. But she was to find out very differently soon enough. We also have a strange, large blue butterfly Natasha continued, which breeds prolifically and has many strange and wonderful facets to its behaviour.

Many have often seen it through the day and it appears to be just a normal iridescent blue butterfly with the same normal behaviour that all butterflies have. But many more folk have seen large gatherings of them near the base of the largest mountain in the country of a night time. They seem to rise to unusual heights and simply fly around and around, the whole time giving off a strong blue glow. Often as they fly in this formation they seem to have flashes and sparks flying off them in all different directions.

I have seen that strange blue light many times, down at the end of the road near my castle Sarsha commented. On some occasions others of the village have seen the flashing blue light as well, and yes it has nearly always been of a night time and occasionally very early morning.

I shall show you in the direction of where I have seen the light Natasha after I have a rest after lunch.

The conversation then flowed happily and strong between the three women about what some of their experiences and past life had been like.

Sarsha mentioned that she had seen many of the tapestries in the palace on the mountain and the fact that she would be now doing some herself considering she was now unable to do physical work to the same extent that she had been doing for the villagers.

After a short while Lenora left Sarsha and the visitor to themselves.

Just before lunch time Lenora, Sapphira, and Beckonny all decide to gather some of the stones which they had been throwing out the back of their now flattened houses and bring them to show Sarsha. When they arrived where the remains of their house were, they noticed the same supply of food which had been delivered so often before, was there again. They still didn't recognise what most of it was but decided to bring that also to show Sarsha.

They arrived back soon after and went out to call Sarsha and the visitor to come and have some lunch.

After lunch the three women brought in the stones and the strange food which they had gathered just before lunch time.

When they walked back into Sarshas room where she was almost asleep the light from the strange stones danced across her room and the brightness from them fully awoke her. She sat up quickly as the three women walked to the side of her bed. Where did you get those beautiful gems she bubbled excitedly? I haven't seen anything like it for many long years. The women explained how they got them and the fact that they did not see any value in them. After all Beckonny proclaimed we haven't seen anything like them, or heard about them so we just thought they were useless but colourful children's stones.

Oh no, Beckonny they are worth more money than you will ever be able to afford if you were trying to buy them anywhere.

How do you know Sarsha? I have seen stones like them in special shops' when I used to live in the places far away from here. They are precious gems which can only be found in a few small places throughout the world.

All of the women were so excited that they forgot about the food which they also brought back from the ruined house lots. What are you carrying under your arms ladies asked Sarsha? Oh dear, this is the food which we have been normally throwing out behind our houses, because we don't know how to use it. They laid it out on the cutting table for Sarsha to see what may be done with it.

I love that kind of food she said and I can certainly show you some great ways of cooking and eating it. They willingly accepted this offer.

After another short time of resting Sarsha remembered that she had told Natasha she would show her what direction of the blue light was coming from. She arose and dressed went and found where Natasha had been talking with the other three women and then took her to see from the gate way of the castle. Natasha was delighted to see that it was the same direction of where she had travelled from, from her own country far away. The two women stood at the gate for a long time sharing their common joy of having seen the strange but beautiful light of the butterflies. Sarsha in particular was quite excited because she now knew what the light was coming from. Her legs were becoming painful again and she told Natasha she would need to sit down again for a short while. At that Natasha left to start her long journey home again and she promised to come again to see Sarsha.

Later that day the three of the women helped Sarsha into a comfortable chair in the kitchen as they all set about to find out how to use and enjoy their unusual provision of food.

Before lunch the following day Sarsha found that her energy level was much better and decided to go with the ladies to the money steward to see if he knew where they could sell the stones.

When they placed the stones on the shiny bench in front of them the steward's eyes smiled knowingly. I can buy all of them Sarsha and any others you may have that are the same as them. What shall you do with all the money? Lenora had been thinking of exactly that since Sarsha had said what they were.

I don't really want to go anywhere else to live because I am happy and content living with Sarsha. What do you think ladies, what do you want to do with the money from your stones. We too are content to stay with Sarsha and not just because we don't pay rent, but because it seems to be a good place to be based while we sew the gowns with Sarshas supply of material and to work on behalf of the villagers. Well said, the steward responded.

Now that I am partly dependant on these women to do some of the work for me and now that they have made it quite clear that they are prepared to work for the benefit of the village and its people, what can be done about changing the usage of the allowance which is here for me to use. I shall speak to Manuel about that Sarsha and let you know tomorrow.

Sapphira then spoke up with the question which still puzzled her from the first time food was left at her place. I still don't know who it was that was leaving the food and strange stones at our place for many years. It was I said the steward. Manuel had given me the stones which he got from his father long ago. The fresh food was delivered to my shop each morning which the columns of light brought down from the garden on the mountain top around the castle there.

I delivered it before sunrise each morning and was honour bound to Manuel not to let anyone know who was doing it unless they specifically asked about it. I have had the money to pay as a good price for the stones whenever anyone brought any of them in here. Until now, no one has done so. Tell the others if they wish, that they too can either sell them to me or learn how to use them to make precious things and sell to the people beyond this village. How is that possible sir, there are no roads for people to come into this village and never has been either. When you all go back to the castle where you are living have a good look at the side o f the road from where the is golden light shining out. He then handed Sapphira, Beckonny and Lenora a large bag of money and they silently left. As soon as they stepped out the door way of the steward's shop they could see clearly the golden light coming from the other side of the road that no one had previously taken notice of. Slowly walking closer to it and examining it carefully they were shocked to see one stone larger than all the rest. Each of them tried to lift it but couldn't budge it. Sarsha bent down and effortlessly lifted it and stood there in shock as she was remembering the first night she tripped over it there. All the women were admiring the glow of the rest of the golden stones so intently that they did not see that they were indeed standing in the middle of a wide and well made road. They did not see that they were being watched by many strangers standing right in the middle of the road directly in front of them.

Who are you Lenora asked with a shrill voice? We are the people who have been trying to come into this village since the times of war and ransacking which we knew would be destroying the homes, farms and killing most of the people here.

But there has been a wall of darkness which we could never understand how it got there or what it was, which rose up after the last time the raiders went through this place.

Lenora then recognised that her heart had been gripped with fear and a cold tightness since she was a young girl and that she had never dealt with it. She could tell by the changing looks on the other two women's faces that they too probably had similar issues to deal with. Sarsha turned to the people standing nearby and asked them if they would first go and talk to Manuel and he would show them how they could best help the villagers. She suggested that they might also like to visit with Leon as well. We have been to see him many years ago they all explained. But when the road way was blocked off we could no longer get through to him. But yes we are more than happy to go and visit Manuel again, is he still the village weaver and do people still go there to receive some of the beautiful gowns and clothing that he makes. No one except Sarsha has been to that shop and received a gown since the wall has been across that part of the road and the village became a cold, mostly dark place. We used to love going to see Manuel and chatting for many hours each time the strangers continued. Sarsha and the others were surprised to hear of this but all remained silent. Come now Sarsha said as they headed off towards the castle while the visitors turned and headed off in the direction of Manuel's shop. Are there any places we can stay in for the night asked one of the strangers. That way we may be able to get started early in the morning with whatever we can do for the remaining people of the village. Sarsha felt further pressure because of the possibility of them asking to stay in the castle because she knew there were no other buildings left that were solid enough for any visitors to stay in.

Trembling inside, she decided to let go of her fear and asked them to come and stay after they had first visited with Manuel.

As all of the women arrived at the castle gate way horse whinnied and raced backwards and forwards from the front of the castle and to the back again. Oh come on horse what's all the excitement about, it's greater than you have been since I rode you at the beginning of my journey to this village? She then touched its nose and he muzzled into her hand.

All the women went inside and prepared their night meal together from the food which had been left for them and had just sat down to eat it when they heard many voices at the door. Sarsha asked Lenora if she could please see who it was as her legs were now so sore that she could hardly stand.

As the seven strangers came in the rest of the castle began to fill with many of the same kind of columns of light as had done so before. All ate with much excitement and happy conversation going on the whole time. During the meal it was discussed what could be done with the money from the stones to help the people of the village. One of the strangers asked if they knew how old the village was. No one knew or had the slightest idea. In fact I don't know how old I am Sarsha said. I have never actually celebrated any of my birthdays in any significant way as long as I can remember. I don't think I have ever done so. Neither have we the three women spoke in unison. Sarsha then went off to bed thinking nothing further of it and slept well the whole night. The other women and the strangers cleared away the dishes from the meal then investigated what rooms could be used to sleep in. They too discovered many other rooms besides those of the servant's quarters which Sarsha had not known of.

The next morning bright and early the women and the strangers were up with breakfast prepared before Sarsha was properly awake. When they had all eaten they shared many high hopes for the village and the plans which they were all prepared to start with straight away. Sarsha went slowly by herself down to the money steward to see what was to be done about the three women being able to access the allowance for the village and the castle upkeep. Manuel was still there in the shop with him. Both greeted Sarsha with a big smile and a hug that left her feeling like a queen for the first time since she came to the village We are proud of your efforts Sarsha to allow others into the castle with you. We know how hard that was for you and how you feel you have lost some of your original freedom because of it. But don't worry, although you will have to make some adjustments to make room for others to have a real say in how things are done now, you will have much to enjoy in other areas you haven't thought of yet. Sarsha prickled a little at that. How dare he tell me what I feel and don't feel? He is getting into my thoughts and understanding me more than I want him to. I shall never invaded you mind in any way that will hurt you Sarsha Manuel said. I shall never betray you or hurt you and attempt to force you to change any of the thoughts that are genuine, real and personally special to you. I shall only ever help you to change what has been harmful to you or to others, but only as you are ready to do so.

The money steward smiled throughout the whole conversation.

The other women can now be free to come and use the allowance as often as it is needed Manuel continued. But tell them they will no longer be getting the stones and the food delivered as previously because it will no longer be needed in that way. The allowance for the castle and village will always be enough to do all that is needed.

Sarsha, you have noticed that golden oil running down the side of the road since the first time you came with me to visit my Father. Now is the time I want you to follow where it is flowing and find out more of what it is about. But can't you just tell me Manuel, because of the growing pain in my legs I am tired of walking and definitely no longer enjoying it. No, this time you must experience it and not just hear about it dear Sarsha. Just believe me when I tell you that the extra effort is going to be well worth your while. I want you to go there early in the morning just as the sun begins to rise and shine on the golden rocks which have been uncovered by the storm.

But can't I be telling the women and the strangers some of the things that are needed for the village and its people. Not any more Sarsha, there are enough people that I have already told what to do. I want you to surrender that part of your life and begin to enjoy the rest of the things I have in store for you, before you go and stay at the castle on the mountain with my Father.

Sarsha was disappointed about the prospect of having nothing specific to do any more in any significant way for the villagers. She felt as though she was useless and that no one had any further use for her, yet somehow a strange peace was building steadily and gently deep inside her.

When Sarsha left the shop Lenora was silently waiting for her. Come she said, wont you allow me to help you get home Sarsha, let me take your arm or even your hand to steady you. She smiled hesitantly at Lenora but did allow her to take her by the hand and thus they walked the whole length of the village street as others watched what they thought was a strange sight. Fancy a woman allowing anyone to help her in that way they queried, after all weren't all the women so used to looking after themselves without a man or anyone at all helping them. Also haven't we women all survived quite well without anyone interference before this? That story and belief of the independence of the village women would begin to change dramatically as the remaining villagers began to see from the very next day. They would come to know a greater sense of community and what genuine help was like as they allowed others to assist them to live a better, safer and happier life style.

Sarsha found it difficult to do next to nothing for the rest of the day. As she went to bed that night she realised that she hadn't told anyone what Manuel had asked her to do the next morning. She was too tired to talk any further and was soon fast asleep.

Early the next morning Sarsha was awoken again by the bright golden light reflecting on the rocks at the roadside. She was soon fully awake and fully dressed and out of the gate way trying to check where the golden oil was ending up. She was too excited and not prepared to wait for any of the other women to bring breakfast in to her or begin to do all the things she had been used to doing on her own. The oil seemed to be flowing a little faster this time as she excitedly set off to follow it. After taking only a few short steps in the same direction as the oil was flowing, there was the boy and the puppy which Sarsha had not seen there for some time now walking close beside her. Can I please walk with you the boy asked? I suppose you can but hurry for now I must keep on going, I have something to investigate.

The three of them followed the glistening oil to the end of the road beyond the castle and around through many smaller hills and large rocks. The beauty and variety of trees and plant life was more than Sarsha had seen or could have imagined in the village. The birds and insects made such a noise as they began to rise for the morning and sing their song of welcome to Sarsha and the boy. The puppy began to chase some butterflies as they attempted to drink nectar from many of the sweet flowers along both sides of the track. After some time Sarsha turned to the boy and said I shall sit here for a while but you may go on if you want to. Oh no, that is quite alright we shall just wait over here under these beautiful trees until you are ready to continue.

Sarsha found a large rock which she thought may have been placed there just for her. She sat there thinking and dozing in the soft, warm sunshine.

After a lengthy period of time Sarsha stirred and was about to continue on the track but noticed that the golden oil had stopped only a short distance from where she sat. She stood and went to have a closer look at it, but realised it was now becoming quite dark and set off to go home again. I shall be coming back here again real soon she thought to herself, I must find out where the oil ends up if possible.

Over the many weeks that followed she spent much time with the three women now living with her, sewing, cooking or simply chatting. Her visits to see Manuel were not as frequent but she stayed longer each time and Manuel certainly welcomed such times as well. Sarsha was privileged to have been there many times when some of the ladies of the village would visit and allow Manuel to convince them to receive one of the beautiful gowns he had tailor made. Her visits to Leons castle on the mountain were also not as frequent because the degenerative condition in her legs. However her visits to Leon grew longer each time. The seven strangers who had come to the village had many lengthy talks with Manuel, seeking counsel for the best way to help the villagers without offending them and how to build the best homes for them. They had begun the rebuilding of the homes with the money for materials from the money steward. Some of the villagers had begun to gather mostly at first for themselves, the many stones which had piled up at the back of their hovels and sold them for materials so the strangers could help them too. After some time they began to sell off some of the stones to help others as well. New shops had gradually begun to be built and many new people came from other villages and had begun to settle into Malkendah. Most of the new arrivals came into the village through the road which was discovered after the night of the great storm. Small trees had begun to spring up at the back of where the hovels had previously been and many of the villagers had begun to grow some vegetables with the seeds the strangers brought in from time to time. Short and decorative fences were being built along the front of the new homes and beautiful roses were being planted and cared for with great attention. The village was taking on the appearance of permanent spring season. Malkendah was now filled with light and warmth and its people were acting happier than they could remember. Most of them had learnt about the joy of receiving a beautiful gown from Manuel and had bit by bit gradually learnt to make clothes for their children.

Sarsha continued her many visits to the new place where the oil seemed to end. But for some reason unknown to her, she never actually bent down again to inspect what she thought was the end of the flow of it for a long time.

Sometimes she would be called to her gate way by other women of the village, who had seen the original dress with its ever changing colours, which Manuel had made for her. Could we too have one they had previously asked? She had promised to do one for all of them with the help of the other ladies now staying with her, but they would have to be patient. She reminded them that the ones which Manuel made were of a greater quality and would last longer, but the women wanted both kinds of gown so they would have a change and would never have to wear any of the old rags which they had been used to for so long.

Night after night Sarsha and the other three women would sit up till the early hours of the morning sewing the gowns for the village women.

Every night as they began to do their sewing of the gowns, many of the tall columns of swaying flashing lights would appear in the rooms and begin their beautiful singing and dancing. Sometimes they would stop just long enough to have given a few words of encouragement to the women as they sewed and then they continued with their energetic celebrations.

Often through those night times of sewing and visiting columns of light, the numbers of women increased who stood at the castle gateway watching the flashing lights and listening to the wonderful music. Yes they continued to watch the increasing activity of the blue light at the end of the road also.

On one of those nights as the women gathered at the gateway with Sarsha watching the flashing lights in the castle and listening to the music, one of the women noticed that the flashing blue light seemed to be breaking up into smaller pieces and coming closer to where they all stood.

As she turned to have a better look there was a huge flash of blue light which suddenly burst outwards and upwards, danced across the sky, stood perfectly still directly above them, then just as suddenly disappeared.

The woman attempted to open her mouth and yell for Sarsha to come and have a look, forgetting that she was already standing there right beside her, but instead the sweetest yet powerful song burst forth from the depth of her heart and filled the air. She suddenly stopped and gasped with surprise for she had never sung that way before. But she vaguely remembered that she had heard her great grandmother sing that way though it was a long time ago and it only happened once. She did not realise that the words of it had remained hidden in her heart all those years since. The other women with her turned to see who it was that had sung such a song. As they turned they too caught the tail end of the blue light dancing across the sky off to their left. They all resolved to tell Sarsha the next morning.

Night after night the music and flashing lights continued. Some of the women began to enter the gateway unasked, each night coming a little closer. One night they found the courage to knock on the doo. Sarsha invited them in to come and have a proper look at what was really making the flashing light and the music. They entered hesitantly and were delighted with the sights and sounds which met them in the great hall of Sarshas castle.

Sarsha could not tell what the time was but knew she was almost falling asleep as she sat in her special chair watching everyone else sewing. Some of the visitors had begun to dance near the columns of swaying light. The original three women began to sing along putting their own words to the strange, sweet sounds that the columns were making. The new visitors had been asking Lenora where she got the beautiful material from, so she took them into the special storage room and showed them. They all came back to the great hall excitedly chattering away. Lenora what has made all these people so happy Asked Sarsha.

Oh Sarsha, they too have seen things which they had only heard about, a long time ago. Their great grandmothers had spoken often of such equipment and materials as they used to spend many long hours sewing with your great grandmother. In the time of darkness of the village they had totally forgotten about it all. Can they come and try to see what they too can contribute for the rest of the villagers. By now Sarsha knew she could no longer fight against the sense of having to release all control over what happened in her castle. She felt that she might as well surrender her previous ideas of doing all the things she wanted to by herself. Her heart settled more especially as she considered the fact that all things being done there was for the benefit of the whole village and not just for the individuals who wanted to take part. She now had the company she had desired and had to admit she was enjoying it immensely.

Sarsha silently walked to her bedroom and slipped into bed and into an instant deep, peaceful sleep.

After that particular night, there was never a day when someone had not gone to Sarshas castle as they sat with each other chatting, singing into the early hours of the night and sewing. Soon they had a large collection of some of the most beautiful gowns that people had heard about in the many surrounding townships. Many enquiries had been made by outsiders, as to where people could get them. Lenora had gone to Manuel and Leon on many occasions to ask what can and what should be done about the excess garments' which were being produced.

The time will come thy both said when you women will be selling them at a price worth their value. Because of such transactions at an honourable price, many more people will come to live in the village to see for themselves what is happening to a place which they had previously considered to be a dead end, cold and dark place not worth visiting. After a short time the many people did come to buy the gowns, to visit Manuel and Leon as the villagers continued to excitedly share about them and the wonderful things on the mountain top in Leon's castle.

Then one morning, again well before daylight, Sarsha could no longer stay in bed and arose, hurriedly dressed and headed off again to track down where the oil ended. As she left the gate horse whinnied and she turned to touch its face as it stepped right up to her. Where are you going so early horse asked? Sarsha was shocked and thought perhaps she was still half asleep. Horses don't talk she told herself. Well, where are you going Sarsha? Oh dear, you really are talking she stammered. How come I can hear you now, how come you have never spoken before she bleated? You were never ready before now Horse explained.

Well horse I am finally going to follow the oil which has run past this gateway for so long and try to see where it ends up. Ok then I shall see you when you return. As she started off again there was the boy and the puppy right beside her as they had been every other morning when Sarsha walked off on the journey of the oil.

The three of them continued for a short while without speaking. Sarsha turned to ask the little boy why he was actually there so often. But the boy was no longer there instead there was a tall dark haired, strong stranger towering above her. He was holding in his hand the lead which loosely hung around a huge, male lion's neck.

Who are you, and why are you here she whispered in total fear and where did you come from? Where is the little boy? Excuse me, but what have you done with him? And on she went with her many questions till she was exhausted. Sarsha, I am that little boy but I have grown into adulthood since I came to Malkendah.I have spoken to you many times as you well know. But you have never noticed how I have been growing taller a little each day since you hugged me that first time in the street. Then where is the little puppy, I miss hugging him? My friend here beside me is that puppy, he too has now grown to full maturity but you can still hug him if you want to. Not very likely Sarsha thought. Oh come on Sarsha; just give it a try as I continue to hold this special tie around his neck. As she forcibly attempted to still her many mixed emotions and tentatively stepped a little closer to lion. Lion lifted his head and gently nuzzled his nose against Sarshas leg. The strength of lion's gentle movement surprised Sarsha and the warmth of his breath on her calmed all her fears. Who are you she asked the stranger, what is your name and where did you come from? I am the little boy which you handed back to the old lady outside that window so long ago. My mother died not long after you had left the village and I had no other relatives left. So, because I had heard about you I decided to follow you and find out what your life was all about. My name is Nivek.I found this lion as a small cub, running around the place where you lived just before the stranger gave you the papers and told you that you were to come here and care for the castle and help the villagers. We have been together ever since. Lion has never learnt how to roar yet and in fact he hasn't made a single sound since I have known him. But Sarsha, why have you been coming to this part of the village so often? What are you looking for, have you found it yet?

Manuel the village weaver told me recently to follow the flow of oil and see where it led to. Because I had already had some moments of curiosity about that, I decided to check it out as soon as possible. I tried to on a couple of occasions but lost concentration and it became dark before I finished investigating it better. When do you think you will actually find out Sarsha he asked? I want to go now and have a much closer look right now, so let us go there and see what can be learnt Nivek.

They set off to the part of the track where Sarsha had sat before on the large rock. I want to sit here just a few moments and simply enjoy the beautiful scenery first Nivek. Have a listen to the sounds of the tiny birds; there are so many different kinds. Their colours are so bright and they seem to move like flashes of light through the branches of these beautiful trees. I have never seen such birds before.

Sarsha, Nivek and lion sat close by each other in silence for a few minutes enjoying the beautiful surroundings as they watched the trees swaying and the birds flitting from branch to branch among the leaves.

Sarsha arose and went towards the same spot where she had seen what she thought was the ending of the flow of the oil before. Nivek and lion watched on but from a distance for a while, then moved closer to her where she was standing on the other side of the road.

As they silently continued to watch, Sarsha bent lower to look at how the oil seemed to drop off the side of the track. As she walked even closer to investigate she stepped on to what appeared to her to be a large rock directly in front of her on the other side of the track.

As she did so the thing began to sway wildly under her weight and she soon realised that it wasn't a rock at all but a large, dense tree. Its outer formation was so dense that unless a person looked really closely they would have believed it to be a rock and not a tree. Sarsha was terrified as she began to fall through the branches at an alarming speed.

Lion roared for the first time in his life but Nivek calmed him as he gently stroke his face I don't understand he said but somehow I know she will be alright now. We will wait here till she comes back up to the top. I believe she will soon find her way back here as we wait for her.

Sarsha was terrified as she continued to plummet downwards. Each move left her with more scratches as the branches tore her skin and her beautiful gown.

The Lion The Mouse And The Eagle

Sarsha came swiftly to a gap in the branches and as she reached out to take a good hold on something solid so she wouldn't fall any further, her heart pounded, her breathing almost ceased, her mind no longer able to make any sense of the present happening, she clutched at the nearest thing. It moved sideways and slid off to a higher branch as the sun caught the bright green colour on its back. No, no Sarsha screamed out, I hate snakes. She hurriedly grabbed at another object which turned out to be a small branch. But it too began to move and creak as her weight strained its attachment to the tree. Let it go, let it go and trust me came a familiar voice from somewhere above her. I can't, I will fall and surely break something she screamed, as the branch began to give way further. Let it go before it is too late came the familiar voice again. At that point Sarsha began to pass out and decided that things couldn't get any worse so she may as well let go and see what happened. Maybe, just maybe there will be someone down below to catch me and save me from being hurt any further. As she let go of the small branch it finally broke off and fell on some rocks below her. A warm wind rose up beneath her and lifted her out from the tree, she put her arms out to try and grab something again but it was too late she was no longer anywhere near the tree. Though she was no longer holding anything and wasn't standing on anything solid yet she felt somehow strangely safe.

She turned her head and saw that she was soaring through some strange kind of a forest or jungle. Wherever she wanted to go, she moved her arms in that direction and they became as eagles wings and carried her directly to that place. I can see differently, I can see the tiniest thing way below me on the ground; my eyes have never been this good.

She continued to soar for some time then began to look for somewhere on the ground where she could rest for a while. She turned her head in every direction trying to find somewhere and suddenly saw a tiny mouse. She also saw a lion which appeared to be crouching not far from mouse as she thought waiting to catch and eat it. I must help the poor little thing she thought. She opened her mouth to shoo the little creature away from the impending danger. But instead a loud screech left her mouth which shocked even her. Mouse had heard that exact sound many times before and was not prepared to wait around to be caught and eaten by such a huge bird as the eagle which was now hovering above it.

I only seem to be frightening him she thought perhaps I had better rest for a short time and try to figure out how to help him better. She decided to go a little higher, perhaps back into the tree again so mouse wouldn't be so afraid. Sarsha eventually rested in the tree which she had previously fallen through and watched mouse. He was so afraid that he hid in a tussock of dry grass only inches away from the crouching lion. I wish I knew how to help she pondered. Come back here came that familiar voice again. Come to the top of the tree and let's talk about it first. How can I come to the top of a tree which has done so much damage she queried? I cannot climb well at all she lamented.

Then a sudden gust of wind caught her wings and lifted her out of the tree once more and she soared to the top of the tree, where she saw Nivek and lion standing on the side of the track, with Manuel now by their side. Yes she commented as she stood beside them, now with normal legs and arms, I thought I recognised your voice just before Manuel.

Come now Sarsha Manuel said, we have a big surprise waiting for you back at your castle. I am not ready for any further surprise at this point she said, and they began the short walk back to the castle.

As they all entered the gate of the castle horse began to race wildly up and down from the front to the back of the castle and back again.

What is stirring him up so much Manuel she asked? Wait and see. Nivek smiled and lion walked softly beside him then sat at the door way as Manuel knocked on it.

Lenora answered the door and smiled broadly, oh great you are home at long last she bubbled. Come and see what we have got as a small surprise. Sarsha could hear many voices in the background behind Lenora. Oh bother she uttered I am definitely not ready for all this fuss and bother, especially dressed the way I am in this tattered gown. Come on Lenora said I will help you get changed and then we shall see what else is happening. Why can't they make up their mind she thought, one is saying a big surprise another is saying a small surprise. Oh dear I am tired enough to sleep for a week she thought. Lenora led her into the small room beside Sarshas bedroom and quickly prepared a hot bath for her. She poured in some rare rose oil and the scent filled the whole room. Where did you ever get such an exquisite perfume Sarsha enquired? Oh that is the oil from the beautiful flowers that have been growing along the foot path from the front door to the gateway.

Manuel showed me how to distil the oil from them. Oh no, what have you done to my precious flowers she cried. Do not worry Sarsha; more will continue to grow as long as this castle exists? There will be many people coming to and fro and shedding many tears which will continue to help more flowers to grow. Did you pick the gold ones as well, yes and that is what has given the gold colour to this oil. Manuel told me that it is the same kind of flowers which have been used and distilled for the oil to flow down from the castle on the mountain to the end of the road where you went today.

Sarsha soaked in the bath for a short while with Lenora standing by the whole time. Why are you still in the room Lenora, queried Sarsha? I do not like anyone with me whenever I bathe. I am only doing what Manuel told me to do. You will understand soon enough anyway. You can stay in the bath as long as you want just ask me and I will get you a towel whenever you are ready. I am definitely not used to all this fussing I wish she would leave me to get on with the job for myself she thought. She stood up and Lenora was instantly there with beautiful soft, purple towel. Stop your fussing, please Lenora leave me alone. No I cannot do that Sarsha, so just relax and enjoy my care for you. Sarsha sat on a small stool to dry herself; her legs had begun to hurt again. For a few seconds only Lenora left the room and was soon back with an armful of what Sarsha assumed was some material from the sewing room. What have you got there Lenora. Be still for a moment Lenora responded I need to do something else first then I shall show you. She stepped up beside Sarsha and began to gently pour some more of the beautiful oil over head and down her shoulders. What on earth are you doing? I am doing again what Manuel told me to do. I haven't done it before, but Manuel said it is called anointing for a queen. I am not any kind of a queen and I don't think I need to have oil poured over me to prove differently. Please be quiet Sarsha we are starting to run out of time now. We need to be down in the great hall in a few minutes. So please be quiet as I do what I have been asked to do for the full preparation of your special time.

Lenora placed the bundle of cloth on Lenora and she saw how beautiful it was. Who made this one Sarsha asked? Manuel made it specifically just for you many years ago. It is called a coronation gown. Sarsha had many questions flying through her mind as she became more agitated. Then Lenora arranged Sarshas hair in a way she had not seen let alone had done for her personally. Then Lenora bent down and picked up the crown which Sarsha had seen the very first day she went investigating the large cupboards of material. I cannot wear that she said, you must Sarsha, it's what Manuel wants for you. But don't worry you won't have to wear it again. Oh good then that's alright I suppose and she quietened down. Lenora, I know my great grandmother was the last queen that reigned here but does that really mean that I still have to dress and carry on the same way as she did. I don't mind working for the villagers but to dress up all fancy like this is not really something I am used to, or had any desire for, or am comfortable with. Just this once Sarsha, just this once is all you have to think about.

All preparations were finally finished and Sarsha found the strength to be silent as Lenora escorted her to the door way of the great hall. As Lenora knocked on the door Beckonny opened it and a gust of sweet perfume, similar to what she had had poured over her, gushed out and all around her. At the same time the room filled with the same music which the columns of light had made many times before. People started to shout and sing spontaneously and Manuel sat waiting for her on the large chair which Sarsha now recognised as the throne. Come now Sarsha and sit beside me. You belong here with me, no one else. All the others have their own special time and place with their own special chair. Tonight it is your turn to hear and do something special. All these people are here at my request, because I invited them. They have come to celebrate your birthday, as they share their own birthday party with you. None of you have known what I can do for you just because I care. Tonight is a new beginning for the whole village. Tonight Sarsha you will see that all those tears you have cried coming up to the door way of this castle have been well worthwhile. Manuel then turned around to the whole room, I want you to remember that all the tears that every one of you have cried and have been collected and I am storing them in a special bottle and one day you will see what has been done with them.

But Manuel, really, can you tell me why, why all this fancy clothing and all the fuss. Sarsha tonight you must decide what you are going to do with the responsibility for the village and its entire people. That is why you have been crowned and dressed accordingly, you are meant to think very carefully, make a judgement and pass a decree that will have resounding effects for the life time of the villagers here and those far beyond. The villagers need to hear what you have decided before we all join in the celebration for all of their birthdays. What do you want done with the castle after you have gone to live permanently at my father's castle on the mountain. If you want to, you can go there quite soon. But for now, make your proclamation and then open the gift that is wrapped up and sits on the arm rest of the chair you are sitting on.

Sarsha sat silently with tears in her eyes. She knew she was getting older all the time but had not thought about much beyond the village and its ever expanding boundaries as all the new people took up residency there.

Of course I want them to feel free to work in the castle to extend in every way possible, the dress making business for the upkeep of the village. I definitely want people to live in this castle at all times, because I do not want to think it may ever fall into disrepair again. I want all the extra rooms which have been found lately to be utilised for all visitors that need somewhere to stay. Especially if they are going to be the appointed workers attempting to do what is truly the very best for this village and its people.

She opened her mouth and began what she now knew was the last time she would speak as she sat on the throne. This is my whole desire for this castle, this village and all the people, new and old, and she repeated her thoughts aloud to all that stood in that room. A roar of cheering and clapping exploded and filled the great hall. Sarsha though she may have also heard the roar of a lion but wasn't quite sure about it. Now Sarsha, Manuel began, open the present beside you on the arm of your throne. She turned and carefully picked up the small package near her. As she opened it all the visitors became curious and silently waited for her to open and investigate what was within. She took from the package a gold ring which fitted her perfectly. There was an unusually large eagle carved from a single dark blue sapphire mounted on the top of it. Now Sarsha, I want you to seal with that ring your proclamation which the court scribe has written as you spoke. He gently took the ring from her hand and carefully placed it on the middle finger of her right hand. She stamped the mark of the ring on the proclamation and all who were there, including the many tall columns of waving, sparkling light began to shout for joy and dance with great excitement. Music filled that hall and flowed out to the village and surrounding mountains in a manner never seen before that time and never heard again afterwards. Sarsha saw clearly that the mark of the eagle was indelibly imprinted where she had pressed her finger. She was drawn into deep thought as she examined the ring closely. Soon, as she watched the ring had completely disintegrated within moments, so she doubted what had just happened, and took a quick glance to see if the marking was still on the document and it was. The great hall of the castle was filled with most of the villagers and some outsiders who had recently come to live in Malkendah. Much dancing and beautiful music continued throughout the night. In the early hours of the morning Manuel suggested that Sarsha may like to go to bed to rest well before her next trip to the new country. But first, please let Lenora help you get dressed in your night garment then bring the crown and your gown with you. I want to take you somewhere in this castle you have not discovered as yet. It is a place of great importance and only specially appointed people are allowed to go. The important thing is that it is only especially appointed people who ever get to visit the place, and then once only in their life time. They are then asked to be silent about what they have seen and learnt in there. Manuel, why is that so important Sarsha asked?

Sarsha dear, if everyone was free to come and go there as they pleased, then the respect and honour for that which is stored in there would lose most of its value. Why Manuel? Sarsha, if people were to enter there without proper preparation they would soon only want to collect for themselves the treasure and riches. They would lose sight of the historical value and disrespect the hard work of those who have gone into that place before them. Then the stored treasures would soon become only as extra finances which would be spent without recognising the value of where it had come from.

Sarsha was humbled by allowing someone else to dress her for bed, as she had been when she allowed Lenora to dress her for the gathering in the hall. It was not something she had let anyone do for her before that night. She knew this night was different in some real way and decided to surrender her battle of independence just to see what would happen. She still had a struggle going on inside her, wanting to do everything for herself, but her sense of safety was growing stronger all the time towards Manuel and she allowed herself to enjoy to some small measure what he had asked Lenora to do for her.

She went back to where Manuel had waited for her as Lenora returned to the great hall to be with the guests. Come now Sarsha Manuel smiled as he took her gently by the hand to what Sarsha thought was only another curtain covering one of the many ornate windows. She had never recognised it as a curtain before therefore; even if she had she would never have pulled it aside because there was already plenty of light in the room. When Manuel had drawn the curtain back Sarsha was shocked to see a small track out into the garden at the side of the castle. The track was overgrown by vines and weeds but not quite enough to totally disguise the bottom of the stair way which was made of solid gold.

Still Sarsha only thought it to be one of the rocks the same as was built into the side of the road which had been recently uncovered by the storm and the running golden oil.

Would you please help me a moment Manuel asked? And they both began to pull away the overgrown weeds and vines. As Sarsha began to pull at the apparent wild grasses she noticed a familiar perfume beginning to spread all around her. Oh I see that you have come to the vine of good health Sarsha. I am happy for you. You shall never be ill again because of the sap which is rubbing off on to you. Soon you will see that your legs will be totally healed and forever all pain will cease to be in them. She was excited about all of that and uttered a whisper of gratitude, but her curiosity was now fully persuaded into full action to find whatever it was hidden behind the weeds. In her effort of weed pulling she became like a thrashing machine. Manuel took Sarsha by the hand again and gently led her up the golden stairway. She was surprised to see the tiny balcony which seemed to be hanging off the side of the wall of the castle. He steadied her as they entered the golden gate which was encrusted with the same kind of gems as was the goblet in Leons castle. The gate way was very narrow; however once they stepped fully on to the balcony she saw that it immediately led into a large hall, greater than the great hall in her castle on the lower level. Why have I never seen this before she asked? Because you were not ready and it was not you appointed time either.

Why is there no evidence of this place from inside my castle Manuel? Because too many people would have found it and made access without preparation and without respect for what lays in there. Sarsha you have still got that perfume on you which were released as you attempted to pull the weeds out. If you had not been prepared to help me with them you would not have been fully prepared to enter here. If people had too easy an access to the place I am about to show you, they would have never known what it was like to be covered in that special oil which you can smell. They would have never been humbled enough to stand in awe of the presence of the greatness of the historical value you are now stepping into and they would have never seen any of the beauty of which you are about to see let alone understand it. At that, Manuel let go of Sarshas hand and took a couple of steps back to allow Sarsha to see and feel for herself without his interjection.

The first thing Sarsha noticed was that this place had no dividing walls and it appearance was of an endless great hall with its boundaries, if there were any, fading off into the distance. How big is this place Manuel? It covers the whole top of your palace Sarsha.

There are no dividing walls because every person that has entered here has always been of equal value. No one person has the right to have any more of a special memorial made just for them. But they all deserve to have equal respect for the effort they have put into the upkeep of the castle and for the work on behalf of the village and its special people. Sarsha also noticed that there were no tapestries or anything else hanging from the walls, but there were long tables as far as you could see and all covered in incredibly beautiful gowns. As Sarsha moved closer to have a better look Manuel asked her not to touch them. Come and I will show you where to put your own gown and crown. They walked together to the end of the room and she noticed a small area at the end of the last table in the room. Oh dear, Manuel look at this gown and she stood still. That one alone you can touch Sarsha. That was your mother's gown. In fact you may pick it up if you are really careful with it. I could never have imagined anything as beautiful as this Manuel, let alone have believed that I could have touched it, and to think it actually belonged to my own mother. She placed it back on the table and stood there sobbing her heart out. She should never have had been allowed to own let alone wear anything as beautiful as this Manuel. She was the cruellest person I have ever met and had done a great deal of damage to many people including myself. Manuel, I notice all the other gowns have a crown right beside them what about this one, is there a crown which should be beside it too? You are holding it in your hand Sarsha. You have worn it once at my request, it belonged to you up till that time, but now what do you want to do with it? Manuel, why should any person who basically lives a life as she did of nothing other than harshness and cruelty towards others ever have the right to wear something as beautiful as this gown and crown.?

Sarsha, remember that I am the village weaver. Every one of these gowns have been made specifically for the ones who wore them at the significant times of making life changing decisions which would affect the people they were supposed to be caring for. No one else would ever be allowed to wear them or use them in any way. Each person has their gown made for one purpose then it is to be surrendered and laid down permanently out of sight of others and to be stored where I and my father alone know where they are. Remember it is I and my father who have chosen all the leaders, kings and queens who have been appointed for the castle of this village. Remember it was we who chose your mother and your other predecessors who would be enthroned for a time here at Malkendah. Sarshas mother's gown was made of dark purple satin with silk panels inserted. The panels of the gown had many precious gems sewn into it and large amounts of fine gold embroidery. The embroidery thread was made from real fine twisted gold. I could never make anything like this Manuel. If my mother had such a gown and this beautiful crown and the palace to live in why was she so cruel and nasty?

It is up top you Sarsha whether you forgive her or not for what she did to you and all the others. But remember one thing; you will never know exactly what she went through herself, with the circumstances of life and cruel treatment from many other people. Such harsh treatment and unjust judgement which helped to drive her beyond all that a normal mother should ever have to do. Remember also she is the only mother that was appointed for you from the beginning. Do you know why the gown of hers is so new looking Sarsha? She never wore it and that was because she always felt that she was so unworthy of such a garment. Leon and I were always watching over her life and helping her in many ways with provision and encouragement. But she never recognised what we were doing and therefore she threw aside most of what was given to her as did the other villagers in Malkendah. She had however in the beginning been able to receive one of the same kinds of gowns as the first one I made for you, but she never wore that very often either. I can no longer remember Manuel, was she tall or short, I think perhaps she was quite short. Pick up the gown again Sarsha and look carefully at it. She did so and was surprised to see how long it was. Are you sure Manuel that this is the exact one made for my mother? I can't remember exactly what she was like, but I don't think she was as tall as this gown seems to suggest. Then Manuel continued in a hushed whisper, my father and I always saw her how she really was meant to be and not through the limitation of clouded eyes like yours are at this time, because of your painful memories of her. Sarsha wept again, I would have loved to have seen her wear this at least once. What about this crown, what should I be doing with it Manuel?

You decide, but would you at least consider honouring her memory and laying it down near your mother's gown on the table? Sarsha timidly placed the crown down near her mother's gown and stepped back to have a better look. The gown and the crown began to shine as if many lights had been turned on in them. The colours of both of them became entwined together like melting glass and danced all over each other and then began to dance up and down the long hall. Nothing else was visible for a long time, except the dancing lights and sparkles of crystal rainbows all around her. You may now want to see the rest of these gowns Sarsha which are actually royal garments. They wandered around looking at all the gowns which had all been specifically made for one person alone. Each one was only ever worn once in the life time of its owner, and that was to pass along the role and responsibility of the upkeep of the castle and the care of the villagers. Manuel shared some of the history of the people who had worn them and then Sarsha remembered hearing about some of it earlier when she was a young girl. She did not like a lot of what she heard that night about all the previous kings and queens. But she did remember what had been said about her mother's struggles in life, and thought perhaps that it was at least some of the same kind of struggles the other regals had been through. But you and Leon have always been watching them and their life too, and you both chose who was to be helper and ruler in Malkendah not I, isn't that so Manuel? Yes. Then I think it's about time I let go of my doubts and fears and give them the respect which they are entitled to, and simply acknowledge their efforts and struggles. I don't have to like them or agree with their life style but they did have a hard job of doing what they were supposed to. Now Sarsha, would you like to consider placing your gown here right beside your mothers gown? She did so and again the lights intensified as all three objects entwined their beauty, colour and sparkling rainbows. New music filled the room with the same sounds as she heard when Leon had handed her the golden, gem encrusted goblet with its special drink that first time in his castle on the mountain.

Oh how she remembered with sweet sadness that time on the mountain top. Now, Manuel spoke with calm authority, you have finally surrendered all the things you felt you alone could control and use or enjoy, before anyone could take them from you or take control over them against your will. But Sarsha, in your attempts to protect them, as you held those things so close to your heart you were actually strangling the very life out of them because you had never allowed any light or life into them. But do not fear, for soon you shall have a rare kind of joy that will never end. You will have a greater freedom of knowing what choices to make and how you can stand in dignity, peace, strength and harmony with other folks as well. You will come to know and accept your true worth to the whole universe and the fact that whatever small or large part you play in it, you are needed to help how it functions. Sometimes you will make decisions that will be quite wrong, but don't become afraid again to the point of not speaking to anyone. It would be good to be careful, and be wise who you share your special times and special treasures with. You can always; learn a right way later if you do or say the wrong thing. You will sometimes make decisions that others will never agree with and in fact shun you from their presence because of how you speak and think. They will not be able to stand having you around them any longer because you will have gone beyond how they understand and therefore beyond what they can control in you or your life. Listen carefully and honestly to your heart Sarsha, it will tell you where to go and what to do in ways that are true to you and for the good of others. Your heart will never know again the emptiness you have had all these years even though you held so many things so close. Be patient and trust me as you wait to see what waits for you specifically, around every bend in the road ahead of you.

Now it is time for you to go and have good night's sleep. I want you to go again early in the morning at sunrise and sit on the large rock which you have done so many times before with Nivek. Sit and enjoy the beautiful scenery as you wait for me. I will show you clearly how to get to that new country that you flew over the top of yesterday. I will show you in the morning how to get down there when you arrive at the edge of the road near the huge rock.

Sarsha and Manuel began their way down the stairway from the room they had been in. As they both continued down each step and leaving it behind, it totally disintegrated. Sarsha had not noticed what was happening behind her as she descended because she thought she had heard a whimper of a small child and was curious to know where it was coming from. As she put her foot to the ground from the last step she thought the sound of the child was right near her and attempted to see where it was. What are you looking for Sarsha Manuel gently asked? I thought I heard a baby cry but cannot see where it is coming from.

Do not concern yourself Sarsha I shall go and find out what is happening while you go to bed and get a good night's rest. She turned to say good night to Manuel and saw that all the steps to the upper room had totally disappeared. What has happened to the steps Manuel? How will others go up there and lay down their gowns and crowns as I have done this night? You are the last one in this particular lineage of sovereign rulers for Malkendah.From this time forwards there will be a different kind of leadership appointed for the job and there will always be more than one at a time to govern, help, protect and love the people. This village is going to be a large city in time to come and now needs a larger group of people to help them with all the changes that are coming with the increase of people and new life style.

Sarsha once more re entered her castle through the same entrance she had come out of behind the heavy tapestry and went off to her bedroom filled with the new thoughts of the many strange happenings in the upper room.

She bent down to take off her shoes and was puzzled when she saw what her shoes were made of. When Lenora had helped her dress earlier that night, before she went to the great hall, she did not notice what was put on her feet but did notice how smooth they felt and how comfortable they were. Now she saw that they were indeed made of solid pearl. When she attempted to take them off they grew over her feet and swiftly began to grow up the full length of her legs. All the joints in her feet became emeralds and her ankles and knees became rubies. When the pearl growth reached her hips, the sockets and joints turned into pockets and solid balls of gold, and there the strange growth finished. As Sarsha watched this strange happening she noticed that the white pearl substance had a soft, pink sheen to it and that her veins had also turned into liquid ruby and glistened as it flowed up and down her legs. Despite the many unusual things which had happened and the lessons Sarsha had to learn that night it was not long before she was in a deep and restful sleep.

Meanwhile at the bottom of where the steps had been Manuel stopped and asked clearly, Nivek what are you doing tonight, here under this beautiful tree? I found this place by accident one day Nivek responded which has sheltered many babies as I have nurtured them as much as possible in this small house which I have built here. I have been many times to the money steward and asked for his help which he gave so willingly with finances and food and clothing supplies. Some of the children I was able to take to other surrounding villages and found homes for them. But sadly Manuel, many of them died because they were so ill when I first found them and are now buried in this small cemetery on the other side of the tree. I am here once more as I have been so many times before with the babies I have found abandoned in the streets of nearby villages. I have often tried to approach Sarsha and ask her help with the care of them, but she has never stood still long enough at any one time for me to be able speak to her about them. How come Manuel she has never seen me here, it is after all another part of the castle grounds. Nivek, no one living has ever found this part of the grounds because the entrance to it has been covered by the thick and fast growing vines. You were able to see this special place because of the many quiet times you spent here walking around after your many visits with Sarsha having tea in her back garden. When other visitors have sat with her and had a cup of tea they always went back through the exact same way they came through from the castle, never investigating the surrounding new areas, never knowing and never finding out what Sarsha would or would not let them do. But you were interested enough in what surrounded that beautiful garden and you took the time to look for different ways of coming and going into such a special place.

I have done the best I was able to Manuel but they have all died at a very young age. Nivek, Sarsha has not been able to deal with any more little babies for a long time. I have been with her when she has tried to nurse many little ones to health. She had never recognised that they were already almost dead, so when they had all died in her arms, she felt as though she was somehow to blame. I knew what was to happen to them but was unable to tell her of it for she would have never understood at the time. In her travelling to this village she has been through many places that were at war. Many of the parents were killed during the battles' and ravages of war. She did try many times to help many babies, but never knew that the babies had only limited time left anyway. But Nivek, this baby that you have here will be quite different for Sarsha wait and see. Give the child to me and I will take care of it from now on. You have done the best you can for many children and now is the time for many others to help in the special work for them. They will come to know what you have learnt and how you developed special ways for children to survive in their young lives and devastating circumstances. First of all Nivek, I want you to share that special knowledge with the women who now work and live in Sarshas castle. Be patient and allow them to develop and train a special group of people who can care for the many abandoned children whether they have a little or a long time left to live. You no longer have to bear that burden alone.

I and my father have watched your efforts and have waited for this time for you to release unto others all the information you've gained from your private efforts of helping so many children.

Nivek, because you have cared for so long about the babies and indeed fort the well being of Sarsha, even when she could not see or receive your love and efforts', I have a surprise for you. Come early in the morning at sunrise and sit on the rock where Sarsha has sat so many times before with you when you walked with her along her new track of discovery.

Early the next morning as the dew on the trees, bushes and flowers began to evaporate in the gentle breeze and the fresh scent of the moist earth rose to meet her nose, Sarsha walked more briskly than before towards her new track and the awaiting large rock. There was no longer any pain in her legs and joy filled her heart in a wonderful but puzzling new way. Horse whinnied at her as she left the gateway and ran backwards and forwards to the back garden and tried many times to jump the fence which held him in such a restricted area. It was obvious he wanted to go with Sarsha one more time. Finally Sarsha arrived at the rock and was delightfully surprised to see Nivek and his lion already sitting there. Why are you here so early she enquired of him? Manuel asked me to come at sunrise so I did was his short and simple explanation. Oh dear, Sarsha said, he asked me to as well just last night outside near the old stair way which I had never seen before. I am sure I had heard a small baby crying but Manuel told me just to go to bed and get a good rest and he would take care of whatever was happening.

Yes Sarsha there was a baby and it was me who had it there. Manuel has taken it and is going to look after it from now on. From what he has explained to me, there is going to be much more care taken of the abandoned and dying children and I am fortunate enough to be able to share some of the way things are to be done. I would love to see more help for the parents who are left in devastating conditions themselves without strength or any means to look after themselves let alone their babies and children. I know there is going to be a lot of work involved but I do believe it is definitely possible to get it started in some real way.

Briefly Sarsha shared some of her experiences of what happened on the mountain top with Leon in his castle. She then suggested that Nivek may want to ask him for some help and directions for the needs of the nearby and distant villagers. He agreed to go as soon as possible. Then they both sat silently and watched the sun rise higher and higher in the sky. Lion sat right at Sarshas side and gently rested his large head in her lap.

After a short while lion turned his head as the trees nearby rustled in the breeze. A low and gentle rumble came from him as Sarsha and Nivek both turned their heads in the direction of the sound and were delighted to see Manuel walking up the track towards them. His smile spread across his face as it shone even brighter than the beautiful sunrise which now filled the sky with glorious colours of bright yellows, pinks and some touches of blue at the outer parts of her vision.

Sarsha noticed that he held some kind of a bundle in his arm but her appetite for the new country was too strong for her to stop and investigate anything else any further. Even though she had so far only sampled a small taste her hunger for more could no longer be denied. She was now consumed with heightened anticipation to start the journey to the new land which she had previously flown over. She did not want to wait another moment to start. She did not want to stop to and ask him what he was holding. Nivek smiled and said nothing, for he sensed what it was that was so carefully wrapped up and held so lovingly in Manuel's arms.

Come now Sarsha and I shall show you how to get to the new country.

Sarsha was instantly off the rock and walking across the track to where Manuel now stood. Sarsha you have two options of getting down there as he pointed to the lower new country.

You can either go down that very narrow track that you see, just near the tree which you previously thought was a rock. If you go that way you need to recognise and remember that there are many sharp rocks which will cut you into ribbons if you fall down them. There are many wild animals, unusual insects and very dangerous snakes, all of which are deadly and have the potential to kill you if they attack. It is definitely very dangerous and just as definitely possible to make the journey that way. Many have done so and survived, they have all been damaged severely and some have not survived because of it.

The other way to that new place is different and it will need all the courage and faith that you have to manage such a way. If you simply stand at the edge of the road here just above the tree, then step off and fly you will get down there safely. But Manuel, that means I cannot hold on to anything or control how fast I descend. Could you control how fast your descent was yesterday Sarsha? You were cut and bruised, your gown was torn to shreds and you were exhausted.

If you take that step of faith and fly down there you will be safe, comfortable, unscratched and your garments will all be intact. I shall be here watching you the whole time and will keep you safe if you just Trust Me. She remembered those words which were spoken to her some time ago and now they rang in her ears with a delightful sound which deeply stirred and filled her heart with joy.

Sarsha remember this, if you take the way of freedom of flight as an eagle would, you will never be able to live on the land and walk like a person with legs again. You shall be able to come to the top of the new country but you shall have to rest in this big tree here and not go back to your castle again. Once you take that last step off the ledge your life will be forever different and your legs will never grow back to normal human legs again. You will never wear those beautiful gowns as long as you are in the new country. You will only have feathers, wings, a large beak and huge strong talons instead of hands which have made so many beautiful gowns. You will always have powerful eyes which can see from great heights and you will always be able to see many things most other people could never imagine because they have never learnt how to soar above the mountains like an eagle.

If you go down there on the track I showed you, you may be seriously damaged but you will be able to return to your palace again and wear those beautiful gowns covered in precious gems. Think Sarsha, wouldn't you like to still be able to chat with the three women now living there and share many hours of working together on the gowns for the business for the villagers.

Sarsha thought about the matter of not having any further fellowship with the other women she had come to now and love and wondered if it was really worthwhile to take the last step and walk, or take the last step and fly. I must be free from this heaviness which is beginning to fill my heart and take a risk one way or another; make a decision and take some kind of action. I know I will miss the company of those beautiful women and of Nivek, Manuel and Leon, but my heart needs to fly now and I must find out what that new country is like and what it is all about.

She took the last step before the actual edge and looked down already having made up her mind to step off in faith and trust that Manuel's words would be real and would actually come to pass.

I shall fly, I shall fly she thought, I won't have to worry about being scratched and damaged any more I shall not have to be concerned about my legs being strong enough or my gown being destroyed either. I will no longer have to be concerned as to how far my legs will or will not carry me.

Just then a bright, deep blue cloud rose up and burst open in front of her. She could now, finally see what had been making that colour fill the sky so many times in the past. There were thousands of large and small iridescent, blue butterflies filling the air and dancing across the sky to draw her attention to the entrance of the new land. Some came and rested on the branches of the large tree near her as the rest continued their aerial ballet. They were now singing some strange song and the occasional word entered her heart{Come now dear one, come now dear one and take one more step where we shall all have fellowship in new and wonderful ways with many others who have taken the same journey before you}Oh Manuel, what do I do, how do I start? Just lift your arms towards the sky and step off the ledge. At that time Lion roared, Manuel and Nivek cried out with one voice {how beautiful, how beautiful she looks}

The Lion The Mouse And The Eagle

Momentarily all the butterflies' had come and rested on Sarshas arms and legs then quickly left her as her large eagles wings formed from where the arms had been and her pearl legs turned into the strong legs of an eagle, while her feet turned into the powerful talons of an unusually large eagle. She had stepped off and begun to soar backwards and forwards in front of them without another hesitation. She could wait no longer and dived swiftly downwards into the forest below her. She was both delighted and shocked to know she could quite clearly see the tiny mouse again just in front of her. She started to swoop to have a closer look and noticed a large lion still seemingly crouched in waiting, ready to pounce on and eat the mouse. I must help, I must help or that poor tiny little thing will be destroyed. She remembered all the other times when she attempted to help small and defenceless babies and cried out in pain at the thought of it. She was shocked yet again at the screech which came out of her mouth, for it was a high pitched shriek never heard from her till that moment. She was only trying to tell mouse to run for his life, but the shriek of an eagle continued to spill from her mouth which had now formed into a powerful, yellow eagle's beak.

Mouse looked up and was terrified when he saw what was hurtling towards him. He hadn't yet realised that there was a lion close by; all he could think of was to escape the talons of the eagle above him.

The mouse scurried as fast as his little legs would carry him towards the forest directly in front of him. Trembling the whole time, totally consumed with fear because of the loud, piercing sound of the screaming eagle which followed right behind him. He was constantly looking back over his shoulder the whole time; to see how close the creature making that terrible scream was getting to him. Suddenly he had been stopped by something huge and seemingly soft, which he had run into even before he was aware he had entered the forest. A rumble exploded all around him, from the depth of that huge mass of soft fur. Startled, the mouse fell backwards on the ground and passed out, no longer able to cope with the ravaging fear that filled his little heart.

After lying on the ground for an unknown length of time, mouse timidly began to stir and look around between the slits of his half opened eyes. Right in front of him were the most gigantic pair of eyes he had ever seen. The mouth right below those eyes was wide open and mouse felt he would drown in them if he went too close. A roar, like the sound of a tornado filled the air and mouse's tiny heart almost stopped beating. He closed his eyes and pretended to be asleep for another lengthy period of time.

The next time he had enough courage to open them half way; he heard two loud voices, seemingly arguing with each other. One seemed to be giving some kind of direction or advice and the other was busy growling and roaring in angry attempts to reject the information. Mouse began to wonder what the problem was with the one who was creating most of the loud noises. Slowly, he completely opened his eyes and looked around him. The first thing he saw was the two giant, sets of yellow claws of the eagle which stood so close and towering above him now. Again He trembled with fear, yet his curiosity told him he was no longer able to put off looking up at the giant bird that stood at the top of those claws and legs. Eagle opened her mouth to ask mouse who he was and what he was doing so close to lion.

At first, mouse could only hear the same screaming sound that had followed him into the jungle.

So he turned to run away again, but the eagle spoke softly and said "Don't be afraid I am only telling lion how to be set free from the thorn bush where he has become entangled, but he won't be quiet and listen. I know he is in pain but he has to be taken out of the thorn bush before he can be free of the pain. "Mouse, you can actually help lion to be free you know"

"Oh no, I certainly cannot and don't want to either, lion will only roar at me and then eat me when I have no strength left to run away from him"

Mouse you need to look carefully at lion to see he is totally trapped and bound up in the thorns of this massive bush. Those thorns are at least thirty centimetres long.

Mouse slowly moved inch by inch towards the two large eyes that seemed to be bigger now than his whole body. Only then did he see that one of those eyes had a large thorn driven right into the corner, while it still remained on the bush. Lion was impaled by the thorn on that bush and it held him close to the ground in such a manner he could not even turn his head.

Slowly mouse walked around the big mouth and saw that some of lion's mane had been pulled over the side of his mouth and held fast to the ground by more thorns from the bush.

Eagle stooped down and picked up mouse and held him carefully in his beak, Again mouse nearly died with fear, but eagle soothed him with clear and comforting words about his safety as longs as he stayed nearby. As mouse calmed down and began to listen more carefully to eagles words he also began to see that lion was in real trouble and indeed couldn't move away from his entanglement amongst the thorns, by himself. Then she carefully put mouse down again on the ground in front of the big mouth and the two big eyes.

Eagle continued to instruct mouse how to help set lion free. However, as yet lion could not see that he was totally unable to set himself free from the pain or from what was causing it. It frightened him to know he was not in control of what was happening to him. Still his pride would not allow him to recognise or accept the help of someone much smaller than himself and therefore more useless as far as he was concerned.

After many days' of arguing about the uselessness of mouse, lion decided to allow this tiny thing do what he was instructed by eagle to do. Mouse and lion had not eaten or drank anything for several days now and the energy and strength of the both of them had run very low.

Still, Mouse began to chew away at the hair in lion's mane and bit by bit the large head of lion was set free. Still the thorn in his eye was holding him close to the ground. Once more, lion roared because of the pain in his head. He was also becoming more afraid with every passing moment that he may die exactly where he was trapped, and of course that made him angrier than at any other time. After all, wasn't he supposed to be the king of the beasts, and of course the king of the jungle? And wasn't he supposed to be master over all that would try to harm him? Wasn't he supposed to be able to set himself free from everything that would trap him into a place of total inactivity and helplessness? Oh well he thought, at least he could still roar and make a big noise to give the impression that he was still somehow in control. But little did he realise it was only making him look like a helpless little creature.

Get this thing out, get this thing out, oh please won't somebody care enough to try and get this thing out. Mouse stood a little closer to lion wondering what he could do to set lion totally free, even though he still feared him. Eagle spoke with a firm but gentle voice, don't touch him yet mouse; you may kill him if you are not careful.

I don't care, I don't care lion roared again, just get it out, now, I beg of you. I can't handle it any longer.

I will arrange what is best for you lion, but you must be patient just a little longer.

I will be back soon and she turned to fly off as the warm wind blew gently under her wings, lifting her higher and higher.

Oh please mouse squeaked; please don't leave me alone here with the one who makes the loud noises.

I know you can do what the lion needs for now mouse, but do not take out the thorn until I return with what you need to dress the wound with.

Oh eagle I am so hungry I haven't eaten for many days now mouse squeaked. I too have not eaten for many days eagle, lion softly moaned, as he began to quieten down.

I know that eagle said, and I do understand how that is making you both more agitated and angry.

With all the pride he could muster mouse stood as tall as his little body would allow. Oh eagle, you are quite mistaken there, mouse squeaked, and in fact I am not really very afraid either. I simply had a temporary shock at the sudden sound of lions roar.

Very well mouse, we shall talk about that some other day. For now you stay with lion and I shall soon be back with the right medicine, and will later go and get you both some food and water.

It only seemed to be seconds before eagle came back with two shells in his talons filled with water. As he carefully placed them both at the feet of mouse, mouse began to drink as though he had not drunk for longer than he could remember. Lion began to groan and moan again and asked where his share of water was. Suddenly mouse realised he had not even thought about the difficulty lion was having in being able to turn his head because of still being impaled on the thorn.

As he turned his head towards lion he heard the voice of eagle pleading with him, mouse, mouse stop, that is to wash the eye of lion before we attempt to take out the thorn. Now move the shells closer to lion's eye and I shall show you what to do with it.

Even though one of the shells was almost half empty; it was still difficult for mouse to move it very far. But with the encouragement of eagle he was able to move it little by little right up close to lion's eye. Then he set about slowly moving the second one closer as well. Every moment he continued to believe he was unable to move it at all. But eagle continually encouraged him to have patience and act in courage.

He wanted them to have the Strength and motivation to continue till the water was close to lion's eyes. Still he was a little puzzled as to why eagle himself wouldn't put the shells with water straight away near lion's eye. The words seemed to become alive inside of mouse and that gave him the strength to do it by himself, instead of asking eagle to do it.

Well mouse, I knew all the time that you could do it,but you had to physically do it to know the strength and endurance you have got within you, enabling you to help others.

Mouse I want you to wet your paws with water from the shells and gently washes away the drops of blood near the corner of lion's eye. Oh, but eagle that will take all day, and really, I cannot be bothered to go so close to one who is going to be roaring and complaining all the time. Mouse, you do not know what will be happening in the future, so trust me, do what I ask and you will be surprised at the results.

Mouse began to wet his paws from the water in the shells and gently wash the blood away from lion's eye.

Mouse I will be back again soon, please keep doing what you are doing till I return. I cannot manage this by myself lion, please help me. You have been shown enough for you to be able to finish the job with excellent results. Don't fret, I will be back soon mouse, then I will show you what to do next. Gradually lion settled down and began to talk to mouse more calmly. He began to realise that if he was to be set free he would need to accept the advice the eagle was giving mouse in how to get the job done.

Mouse, I really thought there would be nothing you could do to help because I am so big compared to you, and you are not really a king or anything like that are you.

I don't know anything about that lion, I only know I can wet my paws and wipe the blood from your eye, just as eagle has asked me to.

Mouse continued wetting his paws and wiping lions eye, but at the same time noticed some of the dirt which he had been covered in, was beginning to wash away as some of the drops of blood from lions eye fell on him.

Soon eagle was back again and this time he carried some strange looking mixture of grass and mud in his beak. Carefully he placed it one of the shells which were now empty. Mouse you have done a good job cleaning lions eye, now it's time to begin taking out the large thorn. First I want you to take small pieces of the mixture and place it carefully around the thorn.

Eagle, what is that strange mixture? And by the way, it really does stink doesn't it.

Mouse, you would not understand even if I explained it to you, some day though you too will be able to make the same mix and use it to dress and assist in the healing of other wounds on other creatures.

Eagle, eagle, look mouse excitedly exclaimed, it is the same colour as the blood I have been washing from lions eye and it actually smells the same too.

Then eagle prompted mouse to get on with the job he had been asked to do in the first place. When mouse had covered the whole area around the thorn with the strange mixture, he stood back and asked eagle, well sir, what is next. Mouse, I want you to close your two front paws around the thorn and gently and very slowly pull it out bit by bit. Remember now, gently and slowly. I am afraid to do that eagle, lion may growl at me again.

Lion, eagle said, I want you to trust me as I direct mouse to take the thorn out. I do not want you to start roaring and snapping your large teeth at mouse. He is frightened enough as it is. Be still now lion and you will soon be free. Lion blinked his one good eye in acknowledgement and lay quite still as mouse began to remove the thorn.

As soon as mouse touched his front paws to each side of the thorn, it slipped out so easily and quickly, that it caught him off guard and he fell backwards on to the ground still holding the huge thorn. Well, lion asked, when are you going to take out the thorn mouse? I have already done so lion. Oh really, well I didn't feel the slightest pain or movement. Please show me the thorn so I can see for myself that the job is finished. Mouse could hardly move with the thorn because it was so large and so heavy. Mouse, I will show it, eagle said as he pick up the large thorn in his powerful beak.

What happened lion, eagle asked why are you caught in that thorn bush in the first place?

Oh, I really don't know. Well, how long have you been there? I don't know that either. Eagle came closer and looked closely and carefully into lion's eye.

Lion you will have to rest for a while because the thorn has gone right through your eye and has scraped the side of your brain. There is some damage there that will need some caring and time for healing, before you are able to continue going through life the way you are really meant to. The damage the thorn has done to you has also caused some serious memory loss. That shall return as you learn anew the things you were taught as a child. You shall grow much stronger in the way you do things from this day forward, because you will feel as though you have been given a new lease on life and all the energy that goes with it. You will be quite surprised at how much others will pay attention to your authority as the king of the jungle, as you learn how to come alongside of those who are weaker than you.

The ones, who seem weakest and most stupid to you, and unable to do anything much for themselves, let alone for you, will need you the most. The ones who seem to be the dumbest are going to need the help of your leadership and authority and great wisdom more than they can recognise at first.

The ones who are the most hungry are going to need your help to learn how to hunt and gather food for themselves, at least until they have gained the necessary skills for themselves.

Oh I don't know about all that stuff, lion groaned. Then stood up and attempted to walk away, before his legs collapsed under him.

Mouse thought he could get away with taunting lion in his time of helplessness, so he proudly stepped right up to lions mouth and squeaked in his high pitched, arrogant little voice, "Oh I see lion, you are after all so weak and helpless, but you now owe me your service and life because I have set you free from danger and possible death." Mouse, eagle spoke sternly, you have no right to speak to lion in that rude manner. You will know times of need for his help even more than you have done for him up till this time. Oh I don't really believe that mouse squeaked back at eagle. Eagle patiently said to mouse, you need to be careful little friend that you do not cut off what lion can do for you in some future day. His strength alone will make possible for you to learn how to survive in times of danger, when no one else is around to help in ways that you may personally desire.

There was something challenging and yet comforting at the same time about eagles voice and words, so mouse stopped talking and thought deeply about the words of eagle. He found a strange quietening happening in his little heart and peace like a cloud of sweet smelling vapours settling on him.

I am still hungry mouse squeaked and I don't know where to even begin looking for food and something to drink. I am too lion said, but with a little more quietness in his voice now.

I will go now and bring you something to eat, but it will be quite different to anything either of you have eaten before.

Again eagle mounted up on the warm winds that seemed to be getting stronger moment by moment. I shall be back soon.

Within a few minutes eagle returned with two more shells the same as the first two he brought with the water in. Mouse and lion looked at each other; silently wondering what was eagle expecting them to do with them. As he placed them on the ground in front of mouse he told him to take out the contents and give one to lion and for him to eat the other. Mouse went close to the first shell and smelt the fish within it and was sick on the spot because of the strange smell upsetting his very empty stomach. Just think of it as a piece of bread eagle spoke gently to him, with the smell of cheese.

Mouse went close again and with his tiny paws worked at the fishy thing till it came loose from the shell, then attempted to eat it again and noticed a small, round, black object stuck in the fleshy part of the fish and stepped back with fear and doubt causing him to silently frown.; What is that thing he finally asked? Are you sure it is not something rotten that may kill me or at least make me very sick. Trust me mouse, I will tell you later what it is, first do what I have told you is for your benefit. Mouse had to go against all of his natural instincts and trust eagle,after all eagles usually eat mice and not feed them, so he held his breath and swallowed the fish, then he spat out the foreign object, because he couldn't chew it.

Lion had become very curious with all that was happening around him and wanted to see what mouse had been talking about. Mouse finally, slowly nudged the second shell nearer to lion and said, "Oh well you may as well have a go for yourself, but be careful about that hard thing stuck in the soft mushy bit". Lion looked and noticed there was another of the black hard things the same as in mouses shell. He began to move his large tongue around and around the fishy thing till it worked loose and he swallowed it without thinking or talking about it any further. He too,like mouse found that he could not chew the hard thing so he spat it out on the ground near the one mouse spat out.

Eagle continued to bring these smelly shells and their contents to mouse and lion until they had eaten enough to feel filled and content. During the time of eating all these fishy things eagle had also ceaselessly been bringing them many shells filled with the sweetest smelling water. But they too had these strange, round black things stuck in the side of the shell that moved free as the water was drunk.

Because lion and mouse had not eaten for many days, because their stomachs were now filled with food, it made them feel so sleepy and content.

Because of eagles wisdom she knew what was needed now to prepare them for the rest of their journey, so she told them both to sleep for a while and she would awaken them when it was time for them to continue on. Eagle went back for a rest at the top of the big tree where she had begun her first flight, and spent some time talking to Manuel and Nivek.

Neither mouse nor lion knew how long they had been asleep but both woke up with a start when a cool breeze began to blow on their faces. They did not move a muscle but looked straight ahead at the incredible beauty of the glorious sunset directly in front of them. They had never seen anything like that before. Where is eagle? Mouse squeaked, and instantly eagle flew right up to the place where they both lay. How come you got here so quickly? Mouse asked with surprise. I heard what you were asking before the words left your mouth little one.

But for now you both need to close your eyes and sleep a little longer. I will wake you up quite soon. It didn't take much convincing for them both to give up all the questioning and wondering, and simply fall back into a deep sleep.

Early the next morning lion and mouse awoke with a shock to the sound of the most beautiful music they could have ever imagined. It was strange music, rather like the sounds of a water fall and the ocean and all the birds of the world mixed together. There was no particular tune they thought, and there were no words they could put together with the sounds they heard to be able to make a song.

As they both lay there slowly and lazily moving their muscles, sometimes they thought they could hear the laughter of little humans. Then eagle flew in from their right hand side and mouse at first did not recognise what or who it was. The sun was rising from behind eagle and she glowed like liquid gold as the sun seemed to run along the full length of her feathers. In some parts, eagle's feathers were like liquid silver. She knew mouse and lion had never seen what was happening so she came quietly, closely to them and stood there a few moments before she spoke again.

Straight away they recognised her voice, which totally calmed the fear that had been rising up in their hearts for some time.

Once more eagle had placed some shells down near their heads where they had been resting. But up until that moment when eagle first spoke, neither of them had realised that eagle had already been backwards and forwards many times, bringing these shells with the strange smelly fish in them.

Come now, eagle spoke with authority and excitement, eat some more of these special fish and then we shall move out of this part of the jungle and see what we can discover that is so close to where you are now. Lion and mouse sensed that there was something quite different about the way eagle was speaking and found themselves wanting to investigate what it was eagle had spoken about that was supposed to be so close by.

Quickly they ate the smelly fish, spitting the small black things onto the ground near the others which they had spat out over the previous days.

Mouse moved closer to eagle and turned his little nose up to eagle and spoke with more confidence that he had been able to up till that time. Eagle I am glad we have had something to eat before we began to investigate the new things you are suggesting, but I have to admit I am still a little bit thirsty, so can we have some water to drink as well please. Eagle just stood there with a huge smile on her face. What is so funny lion enquired? After all, mouse only asked for some water to drink. Oh yes that's true lion, but for the first time since I have been talking to you both, no one has ever said thank you for anything. So you see I am happy to know mouse is beginning to see how good it is to be thankful for what is being given to him.

Mouse, when we start to investigate what is around you, you will come to some of the sweetest water you have ever tasted, but this time you will be able to get it for yourself. Mouse had some mixed feelings about all that, he had become so used to eagle bringing his water and food for him, he had lost all confidence in himself and doubted that the little bit of knowledge he had would be of any use. Even though mouse did not speak his doubts aloud, eagle knew exactly what was going through his mind. Don't worry mouse; you will find it easy once you begin to do things for yourself again. Lion sat there silently, because he was beginning to think the same things mouse was. Both of them knew, eagle really did know what they were feeling and thinking but did not have the courage to ask how she knew.

Lion and mouse both stood up and stretched their bodies and began to walk towards eagle.

Oh come on now, are you really going to leave those black things behind you, lying on the ground, as though they had no value at all. This time their curiosity and their lack of any sense of value towards the black things opened their mouths at the same time, "What is the use of bringing those useless things, and besides, what shall we carry them in eagle?"

Both of you have a look under the fur that covers your chest and you will find something there big enough to carry everything in it that I will ever give to you.

They both thought eagle was a little bit crazy now, after all didn't they both know their own bodies well enough to know what was under their fur, and know it better than anyone else could possibly know. However, they did run their paws through the fur overt their chest and were totally shocked to find there was a strange kind of a small, heart shaped bag hanging there, which they had never seen or felt before then. But they are so tiny nothing will ever be able to be put in that, let alone all those black things. Once more eagle just stood there with the warmest smile on her face.

Come now, put the black things in the bags and we shall head off to see what I have been trying to tell you about. Lion and mouse were surprised to find as they put the black things one by one into their bags, the bag grew just big enough to make room for the next one.

They began to become afraid again, because they thought the bag would become so large and heavy that they would not be able to carry it around. Both of them began to attempt to take the bag off their chest, but found that it was somehow stuck to them. Don't try to take them off, eagle whispered; you will destroy yourselves if you do. They are actually a part of you in fact you could say that they are the heart of everything good that you do.

They were not used to eagle speaking so quietly, and so made out they did not hear him and continued to try and take them off. Again and again eagle whispered; don't do that you will harm yourself. After many times of softly whispering, they had to acknowledge eagle was speaking specifically to them and maybe, just maybe she knew what she was talking about, so they stopped struggling to remove the bags on their chests.

Ok. Now are we ready to go ahead Eagle asked? And then lion and mouse stopped fussing and began to walk in eagle's direction. Eagle suddenly lifted up and soared above them. Please don't go too far away they pleaded, and why can't you walk on the ground like us anyway?

Eagle whispered again "I shall always be with you, to tell you what way you should be going and what the best thing is to be doing, but you will need to slow down and listen carefully to be able to hear me clearly.

Suddenly they realised, where they were walking was much brighter than where they had been for the last several days. I feel quite strange lion, mouse squeaked. Yeah me too mouse and suddenly they realised they were talking to each other as if they had been the best of buddies and had known each other all their lives.

Although Eagle may have been soaring high above, she could still see and hear clearly, everything they were saying and doing, and again she just silently smiled.

After walking just a short distance they began to run faster than they had previously thought possible. It was as if they had just had a massive weight suddenly lifted off them.

Lion, lion, slow down I cannot keep up with your mouse squeaked. Lion continued on as though he had not heard mouse squeaking and pleading with him to stop. Suddenly something with four large legs knocked mouse off the side of the road into a rock at the side of the track. It happened so fast that mouse couldn't see what it was.

Finally lion realised he could no longer hear mouse squeaking; reluctantly he turned to see where mouse was he was ready to roar in anger at mouse for going too slow.

But when he saw him laying flat out against the rock his heart stirred a little with compassion and he went back and gently said to mouse "Oh O.K. mouse, come on climb up on my back and I will carry you for a while.

Mouse then felt as though some memory was trying to rise to his mind, but he was too excited to pay it much attention.

Eagle whispered for them to be careful where they were running. He knew they were headed for a large pit up ahead which some hunters had dug only the day before, to trap many different wild animals for the zoo in another far away land.

Then lion ran as though the wind had lifted him too off the ground and was carrying him like a small leaf.

Hey lion, I can smell something strange and beautiful, can you smell it too? I sure can said lion as his speed continued to increase.

Eagle continued to whisper his warning to them but they could no longer hear her. They temporally forgot she was soaring directly above them.

Suddenly, they saw many other lions, and elephants and zebra and antelope speeding past them, coming from the direction they were headed towards. There was so much dust it was difficult to see clearly how many there were, but they seemed to be racing past for the longest period of time.

There was a strange thing making a lot of noise carrying some even stranger looking creatures which were making a lot of noise as they followed close behind the racing animals.

Lion was not interested in stopping but asked mouse what he thought all those strange things were in the racing thing.

Oh I believe they are called humans he squeaked, and the thing they are sitting in I believe is called a truck. I used to stay in the humans houses sometimes when the weather was getting too cold and I could find no food for my family. Often I would sneak up and sit in the cracks of the boards in the floor close to their fire and warm myself there till the morning. I would often hear the people talking about how their trucks would make a lot of noise while they were hunting the animals. I never knew what hunting really meant, but I think what is happening now would be called hunting.

After their fire would go out I would begin to feel the cold and awaken again. Because the people had gone to their special rooms to sleep for the night, I was free to hunt for any crumbs of food on the floors and take them to my family.

However, one morning I awoke a little later than usual and smelt some smoke and sneaked out doors to look at what was happening. The part of the building where I had built a nest for my family was burning and the humans were just standing there talking and laughing. I was puzzled why they were not trying to put it out.

I ran as fast as I could towards where my family had been living but by the time I got there, it was too late, everything had simply collapsed into a heap of burning ashes.

Later that night when I sneaked again into the human's house and snuggled in the cracks in the floor boards, I heard them saying how good a job they did in getting rid of the useless old building so quickly. They were pleased at the swift work of the flames as they totally consumed the wooden structure, but they didn't know they had also burnt down the nest of many of the families of my relatives as well.

I decided after that I would have to go somewhere else to live and look for new things to do, because I no longer wanted to have any more family that I could not protect.

I had been living from that time onwards in the high grasses and enjoying the seeds and different grains of the fields as I travelled.

Lion that is how I bumped into you the way I did. I had been slowly been going out further and further, heading off to a new field each day. Not caring in which direction I went, as long as I never again had to live in a place where humans had built the places they slept in each night. But the further I got away from the humans buildings, the more I saw and heard those terrifying sounds of eagle. I had never seen or heard such a thing when I was near the human's houses. Then one day I heard eagle close behind me and I was afraid to stop running, even though I could not see properly what was in front of me. Suddenly I bumped into you.

Suddenly lion saw the truck was only a few metres away from where he and mouse had been standing and talking. Come on, come on mouse get on my back we have no more time for idle chattering just now.

Mouse scurried up onto lions back and held on to lions main as hard as his little paws would allow him to.

Lion took a sharp turn left and entered again into another part of the jungle that they had only left a few minutes earlier. Only then did he and mouse realise how thick the undergrowth was among the trees and bushes and exotic flowers. Many different kinds of birds scattered throughout the many tall trees all making their distinct yet harmonising sounds at the one time. Monkeys chattered like a million people all at the same time, as lion sped past with his tiny passenger clinging tightly to his hair. Lion soon came to a clearing in the jungle and decided to take a careful look to see if it was safe to continue on the track he had originally begun on. He only paused for a few moments and then started to run again in the open road.

Hey lion, there seems to be something missing, what is it do you think? Suddenly at the same time they both remembered that there was an eagle with them when they first started to move out of the jungle. Mouse indignantly stood tall again on lions back and begun to grumble about eagle taking off without at least first saying goodbye.

Lion, lion, stop right there eagle screamed. Lion didn't hesitate this time; he sensed the urgency in eagle's voice. As he stopped he saw that he was indeed right on the edge of the biggest hole he had ever seen. Why didn't you tell us about this great hole well before now lion pleaded? And now that I think about it, where were you all this time when the animals were racing past and that strange truck was coming towards us with all its noises. Lion I have never left you and I have been trying to tell you about it since you left the jungle, but you were not listening during your time of hurrying ahead, eagle spoke quietly.

Oh I see said lion, well I guess I had better try and take a bit more notice in future hadn't I.

Come on now eagle said as she began to rise up with the wind which gently stirred the trees and bushes nearby.

Without hesitation and without asking questions this time mouse instantly scurried up on to lions back and hung on to his mane. Within moments they had moved off further down the track at the side of the jungle where they had just come from.

The sounds of the strange truck thing had move out of sight and the many frightened and noisy animals were also out of sight and beyond the hearing of mouse and lion

Mouse asked will the next place we go to be the same as where we have just come from lion.

Eagle flew a little lower towards them both and quietly but joyfully spoke to them both at length about what they were about to enter into. It sounded like the sort of place anyone would want to live in for the rest of their lives.

Oh no mouse you will only be there for a very short time, it is just the place of preparation for things that you haven't even began to think about yet. You will need everything that you see and hear and collect for the next part of your journey.

Because the track had gradually begun to turn off to the left, mouse and lion hadn't realised that their direction was changing at all until they came suddenly to a place beyond their imaginations. They could hear the strange and beautiful sounds of many exotic birds, totally different to the ones they had for a short time heard back in the other section of the jungle.

Then they found themselves in the middle of a clearing in the new section of the jungle. Running through the end of that clearing was a beautiful little brook with crystal clear water bubbling with sounds like that of little children laughing and playing.

Lion instinctively ran towards it as mouse squeaked hurry, hurry I want to see what is making all that beautiful noise.

As they stopped at the edge of the brook they saw tiny little birds and many different kinds of butterflies quietly standing at the water's edge sipping the sweet moisture.

Mouse was surprised to see how still they seemed to be, and how they didn't run away when lion began to roar with joy. In fact some of the little birds hopped closer to him all chattering at the same time. Slowly, it was clear they were actually talking to them and showing real joy at seeing newcomers in the same place where they too had found so much joy and peace.

Why didn't you little ones fly away when I roared before?

Why should we, we don't fear you in any way. Are we supposed to be afraid of you?

Normally the creatures of the jungle are frightened of me, especially the smaller ones.

Well lion, we have not been told about such things, you are welcome here as long as you don't try to destroy us or our other friends or the jungle around you.

At that time many spotted deer came up to the water's edge and began to drink until they saw lion standing there, then they swiftly ran off without asking questions.

They are scared of me lion exclaimed, I wish they too could feel comfortable like you do in my presence.

Just be patient lion, they are timid creatures by nature and they have been pursued many times before and many of their family have been caught and eaten by other lions. But if you wait here patiently till the sun has finished setting, you will see them return, because this is the only water hole around this area.

As the suns final rays settled over the tops of the giant trees, the deer timidly came back to the water's edge and tentatively began to drink again.

Many of the birds hopped over near them and gently spoke to them about how lion and mouse had come for a short visit. They spoke also about how they had promised not to destroy them or any of their families.

As lion and mouse lay quietly off to the side amongst some tall grasses, they wondered at how the chattering of the birds had changed so much, it was now distinctly a proper conversation which they could both understand quite easily and clearly.

Then after a lengthy time the birds hopped back to where lion and mouse lay resting. Soon they realised that the sounds of the birds had changed back to understandable conversation again.

One tiny little blue bird hopped close and whispered, come lion and I will introduce you to some of my special friends.

They are a little frightened because other lions have pursued many of their relatives to the death, many times before. I have assured them that you will not try in any way to destroy them, so instead of eating them as is the normal thing for lions to do, can you be patient and wait till we can get some other food for you to eat?

This entire time mouse was wondering what he was supposed to eat. He was not able to hunt larger animals, and even if he was, he was not sure he would enjoy ripping apart and chewing into anything that had blood dripping out of it.

He didn't want to look like a fool so he didn't mention his puzzling thoughts to anyone else.

Then, as if some of the birds could hear what he was thinking, they hopped closely to mouse and asked if he would like to come and have a look at some of the things which they had gathered during the day. Mouse followed quietly, wondering the whole time what these little birds could possibly have gathered to eat that he would in any way be interested in.

He was shocked to see, not far from where he had been laying with lion, a large stump of a tree that had been blown down. Some of the birds explained that the tree had been blown down by a bad storm which had ripped through that part of the forest many years before.

On top of this stump were the most luscious berries, nuts and fruits that any small creature could imagine, including this one small mouse? As he approached the stump to investigate further, he was wondering how he would get up to the wonderful feast he imagined was waiting just for him alone.

A quiet, deep voice behind him said "Hey wait on a minute, what do you think you are doing, don't think you are going to steal our food from us when you think we are not looking"

Mouse spun around to see a large monkey standing right behind him.

Oh I do wish people would stop creeping up behind me and frightening the living daylights out of me, mouse thought. Then monkey stepped right up to him and took mouse in his hand and lifted him onto the stump top and said go on now, eat as much as you want, I was only joking, I knew exactly who you were. The birds have already told me that you have been invited to share our tea with us. We always gather food for a celebration feast each night. Thank you so much monkey for sharing your food with me. But why do you have a celebration feast so often.

Well, you see it is like this old man monkey said as he sat down near the stump. All of us in this little community have come from many different parts of that very large jungle. All of us have been hunted to be killed or sold to wealthy humans that want to keep us locked up in cages, so other people can pay money to come and see us.

Oh really monkey, squeaked mouse, that hardly seems fair, you are the ones who have your freedom stolen from you, and then locked up in cages. Yet it is the humans who get money from other humans to come and stare at you.

Well mouse, that is exactly why we all celebrate together, for we really do appreciate the freedom we have here, and we never know when it will be one of us next who is captured and locked up in a cage. So we celebrate as often as possible to encourage each other in what we have as our precious freedom to be and do all that we need to, to enjoy life and help one another, especially with gathering the food we need.

You see mouse, each one of us can gather different kinds of food than the others do. We have discovered that some of what others eat is safe and enjoyable for us too. So we share and make it an adventure as we learn about some of the different ways to mix our foods with some of the foods of others. It is quite surprising at times the amazing flavours and combinations of recipes we can create, and each and every one of them quite enjoyable I must add.

Suddenly mouse realised lion was no longer with him so he began to be a little frightened, after all he was very used to lion being there with him at all times in the last few weeks.

I really want to go and be with lion please he stammered. Don't worry mouse he is not far from here and he too is doing some new things, but we shall all be together in a few minutes.

Mouse suddenly spun around at the sound of loud laughter mixed with an unusual roar which seemed to be coming closer and closer all the time.

There right behind him stood lion with the biggest smile on his face.

Oh mouse he exclaimed, I did have the greatest time with all the new friends I have found amongst those who were only strangers before. Some of the things they did truly brought joy and an abundance of laughter in ways I have never had before.

I also have learnt to roar in a way which I had forgotten about for a long time.

Oh mouse you should really have heard the funny noises some of the deer make as the little birds hop around their ears catching all the little insects trying to settle in their warm fur.

Mouse settled down again at the sight of his friend standing right beside him. But he was a little worried at the sound lion had made as he was coming closer up behind him.

I wonder said lion, do you think mouse it might be time to continue on with our journey now, or should we wait a while and see what happens here first. Well lion, I feel it is too dark now; we would really have to wait till the morning at least to see clearly where we are going.

So let's just stay here a while enjoying this part of the jungle, that is if the other animals and birds don't mind.

Oh please stay with us as long as you want, some of the birds chattered in unison.

Mouse was thrilled at the invitation for it was a long time since any one had asked him to stay with them. So they all began to settle down for the night in the thick bushes where it was warmer and more protected from unwanted visitors during the night.

Mouse was then surprised at how easily all the birds just seemed to open their wings and the next moment they were all perched on branches with their heads tucked under their wings and fast asleep.

Finally he and lion had settled amongst some finer ferns not far from the big stump which had been covered with all the different fruits and berries for the community tea.

Lion had such a good time with all his new friends and had not forgotten how much fun he had as he ran and played with them all. He was so tired, he hardly had time to put his head on his paws and he was fast asleep. Because mouse was still trying to get used to all the new friends and strange happenings, he took a little longer to settle the feint fear which was attempting to fill his tiny heart again.

Finally he crept right up to lion's mane and snuggled into the warm, long hairs of lions crowning glory.

Early the next morning as the sun rose and all the birds began their bright chattering, and the animals began to stir and set off for their day of adventure and hunting for food, mouse stirred from his deep sleep with the gentle touch of a large butterfly brushing backwards and forwards across his tiny nose.

Oh dear me what is that tickling my nose lion can you see? There was no answer. Lion are you awake he asked. Still there was no answer. Mouse stirred more now and wondered what it was that still tickled his nose so persistently.

Then he realised lion wasn't even there, he had gone to have a wander around this beautiful new place which they had been invited to stay.

Suddenly old man monkey started screeching from up high in the trees where he had slept for the night. Mouse, mouse, you need to move there is a snake coming right towards you, it is so large it will swallow you in one go if it catches you. Mouse jumped right off the ground with his little heart thumping even more than when eagle gad come up behind him screaming so long ago.

As he scurried further into the bushes to hide he noticed a beautiful, bright blue butterfly flying just above his head. As mouses heart began to settle down he could actually hear what seemed to be a whisper saying come this way, come this way and you will be safe. It took a while for him to realise it was actually the butterfly. He never knew before butterflies could talk, and in fact he had never seen a butterfly so close to him either.

Suddenly old man monkey was right beside him, grabbed his tail and swiftly climbed up the big tree with him where he had been sleeping. As he did so, the monkey told mouse to look down near the spot where he had been laying with lion during the night. And to his amazement there was a giant of a snake slithering around and hissing in anger, he had been deprived of the morsel of food which mouse would have been.

Oh beautiful butterfly, thank you so much for warning me of the large snake that was creeping up to eat me. He was so silent; I would never have woken up in time. But because of your gentle touch to my face, which helped awaken me I am now safe. Then, oh yes and then when monkey picked me up and took me to safety high up in the tree, I began to appreciate my freedom much more and now I am now able to enjoy this beautiful place a lot longer.

Butterfly smiled gently and shyly flew to a branch a little higher than mouse and sat there watching everything that was happening below. As she flew upwards her wings spread out like a mighty kite and everyone was amazed at how big she then looked. Mouse could see all the beautiful colours of shiny blue, pink lemon and soft green, all running in together like a cloud of soft water hanging in the sky., underneath her wings as the sun shone through them. The sun glistening on what appeared to be tiny diamonds that gave off the effect of sparks of fire. As she flew past him many times he noticed that the mixture of colours was on the underneath and the iridescent blue was only on the top side of her wings.

Mouse let out a little squeak of pure delight and asked her where she got such beauty from and why couldn't he have the same colours over his dull grey, furry little back.

Oh mouse you are fine just the way you are at the moment. When we are born we all have the best kinds of bodies that we need. With just the right size, shape and colours that we will make the best use of as we simply live the lives we are meant to.

As we go about doing the things that are true to our heart, all the different movements of our bodies will place us in just the right angle in the light of the sun, to show off our true colours and marvellous structure. When we are living in that way, many people will also look at us and ask the same kinds of questions as the ones you are asking me now mouse. But that is only because they have lost all confidence in themselves and all their truthful perception of the beauty and greatness of which they were born with.

Mouse, when we are looking too far outwards beyond ourselves and looking too closely at what other people are doing and how they seem to appear to us, we lose sight of what we genuinely are and what we are supposed to be doing as individuals

But what am I made for butterfly, and any way what is your name, do you have any special name? Yes little one my name is Pricilla. Even your name is beautiful Pricilla. Thank you mouse, and what is your name well, I shall have to think about that for a minute, it is such long time since I have heard anyone call me by name. Yes that's right, I remember now, I remember when my mum used to call me for lunch. She used to call and call and I would hide behind the huge berry bush near our door way. Monty, Monty come on inside or you won't get anything for lunch. I was often much too cheeky and sometimes I would not answer straight away, just to see how upset she would become before she gave up and went inside again. I did miss out on food sometimes, but soon learnt to go out and hunt for some seeds and things in the large garden around the house.

I can remember one time in particular when I was wandering away from my home when a Falcon flew down and picked me up by the tail and began to fly away. I began to squeak and squeal and fortunately my mother was nearby and began to bite into falcon's leg and he instantly dropped me.

I certainly scurried inside then where mother had some unusually large berries waiting for me. They seemed to be the tastiest ones I had ever eaten up til that time.

Pricilla, you did not give up on me when you kept on calling me to come this way to be safe, I am so thankful for that. It is strange though, you don't really have a loud voice or anything like that but I knew exactly what you meant, why is that possible?

Little Monty, when someone loves you with a pure and true heart you can get to know what their intentions are sometimes even when they are not speaking words out loud.

Priscilla, why do I feel as though I am somehow older now? Oh Monty, you have grown up a little more, which shows me your heart is still tender enough to be able to learn new things about yourself and the world you are living in, and the people that share it with you.. But remember little friend that we need to be ready to be learning every day of our life or we shall become too hard and nasty and proud and we will be hurting others with the way we act or speak.

Monty began to look around and saw that there were many clouds building up above the tops of the tall trees. Thunder began to crash and lightning cracked close by, again Monty thought he could hear the sweet whisper of Priscilla and turned to listen more carefully. I must go now Monty, I shall not be able to fly if too much water gets on my wings. It is time for you to continue on with Lion now. Also remember little friend, just be what you know in your heart is the real you, then she seemed to disappear instantly. She was gone and Monty was missing her already.

Monkey had been happy enough to sit in the trees above, grooming himself and eating some luscious berries that had been left over from the feast the night before. But now he could see the storm that was building up close by and knew,mouse would be in trouble if he did not soon prepare to go on to the next place with Lion.

Old man monkey became quite restless as he began to chatter endlessly and Monty was angry for a little while, he had forgotten that it was he who took him high up into the tree to safety. I am sorry monkey, I was just missing my dear, pretty friend, and how she was so good to me.

Don't forget Monty, you do have other friends too, even if they show their care for you in different ways than Priscilla did.

Monty shared with monkey how he was grateful for being taken to safety, but in the beginning was a little frightened at being picked up by the tail. It reminded him of how frightened he was and what it was like when the falcon had picked him up exactly the same way so long ago.

Lion entered the round patch of forest where Monty had spent such a special time with his lovely butterfly friend. He was a little frightened at the appearance and sound of Lion for a few moments, until he remembered that Lion too was a special friend, which he had desperately missed when he first went away to investigate the surrounding forest.

Old man monkey was now on the ground right near Monty and was gently touching his hand as he was saying good bye.

Come on Monty, come on we must go now or we are going to be in real trouble very soon. Come on get up on my back again, we have to get going, now.

The birds and other animals which had so willingly and happily shared their banquet with mouse and Lion, began singing out and chattering as they too said good bye and quickly settled in, in the protection of their nests, and hidden pockets among the trees, bushes and small caves in the forest. They knew there was an unusually powerful storm coming and they certainly wanted to be safe till it was all over.

Mouse scurried up on to Lions back and spoke of how he had originally been so afraid and felt so abandoned when Lion first left. There are many times Lion when I am afraid, I don't think I have much courage like you or, monkey or even like Priscilla.

Monty, you are on my back now aren't you? Yes. Well hasn't that taken a lot of courage for you to do that? Oh, yes, but I forgot.

Why can't I have big courage all the time Lion?

Monty, remember that you are indeed a tiny little mouse, and for such a small creature you actually have the courage of a giant.

Monty, it takes a brave creature to look at things which are going to happen often in our lives, which can cause us to be totally afraid. But it makes our courage grow each time we decide to go ahead even though fear grips our heart like a hungry creature. So, when we are acting with courage we will actually forget how big or how small we are. Courage itself is a mighty force Monty when we put it into action and then it looks bigger than all else around us.

A few large drops of rain began to fall on Lions back and mouse was surprised and sat there in awe. Monty I think you should get underneath my hairy mane so you won't get too wet up there. Monty scurried under the warm mane and Lion began to quicken his pace as he ran out of the clearing in the jungle.

Why are you in so much of a hurry Lion? What seems to be the matter?

Monty, when I went off to investigate the rest of the forest, I discovered that we are actually on a small island. We have come across a strip of land which is connected to the rest of the main land. In our excitement we had not recognised that we were going towards this island. The storm which is now beginning to break free is coming from the direction of the main land and we are unable to go back that way, because it is so powerful. We would not have the strength to go against the storm.

Right at that time, they could hear the distinct scream of eagle high above them. Come on you guys, come on, you are going to be in trouble unless you are clear of this place very soon.

Mouse peeped out from the cover of lions' mane, and was amazed to see how high eagle was up in the sky. Why are you still up there eagle? Why are you going right through all the clouds and thunder and lightning? I am hiding from it here under Lions mane, and I think that this is warmer and that it is a much better place to be.

Monty, I cannot explain to you why I am doing. All I know is that it is how eagles have always done things when a storm comes. The power of that call to climb higher is so strong upon our hearts that we eagles can only respond to it by rising way above where the storm is raging through all that is around us, without questioning where it comes from. We eagles have never been able to resist looking for the one who is behind the voice which calls us to go higher so we just follow what it tells us, because we have come to know that voice always takes us to a safe place. I know one day if we keep going towards that voice each time there is a storm we shall be safe, and then one day we shall see the one who calls so strongly to come and go right up through the storms. I also know when the storm is over I will be able to tell you where you can go for cover and to find more food to eat. Every time we eagles go above the storms we also see much clearer what is below us. When we are walking on the ground or eating on the ground we can only ever see a very limited area around us. When we are soaring above everything below, then we can see for many miles in all directions.

Not even Lion can do that.

We are all made differently, and all have something uniquely powerful and beautiful within us.

Oh yes, that's right Lion, Monty squeaked, I remember now, that's the same kind of thing which Priscilla butterfly talked to me about when I questioned why she was more beautiful looking than I am.

The temperature was becoming colder by the moment. The rain was beginning to lash at lions face as he sped onwards, towards what he thought was a safe place. He could no longer see where he was headed but just kept on going at full speed. He could no longer clearly hear any of the words eagle was screaming out to warn him that he was going in the wrong way and was headed for serious danger.

It seemed like hours that Lion had been racing forwards. His legs were becoming weaker by the moment, he no longer had clear visibility, and to add to the confusion, Monty was so terrified and had begun to squeak ceaselessly.

Oh Monty, please try and be a little quieter I am dong the very best that I know how to get us both to a place of safety and warmth. Perhaps you would be little more comfortable and feel a bit safer if you travelled inside my ear for a while.

Monty instantly darted into the right ear of Lion; he didn't have to hear or argue with that invitation twice.

Lion could no longer hear anything except the sound of his own heart pounding inside his chest. His legs were now moving like robots then suddenly he could no longer feel the ground under his feet. They were falling in a watery uncontrollable rush as the driving storm swept them faster and faster downwards.

For a few moments Lion had passed out and indeed had begun to drown. Mouse no longer had the energy to squeak and had no idea where he was or what was happening. The only reason he was still able to stay in Lions ear was because he had become entangled in lion's hair near his ears.

In between moments of unconsciousness and being alert Lion began to listen to the roar of the water all around him but wondered why he was unable to breathe properly without water rushing into his mouth. Suddenly he realised that he was indeed in some kind of deep cold and dark water which was swirling, rushing, and tossing him around like a leaf.

The more he tried to have control of where he put his feet the harder it was for him to swim in that tumultuous grave. He soon realised that all he could do was try and come to the surface of this watery place and have a look around to see where he was.

He kept on swimming as best as he could while the water around him was weighing down his wonderful mane, which he had been so proud of previously.

The water got colder and colder. Lion didn't realise that for a time he was being dragged deeper with every movement he made. He had been under water for a long time and now his lungs began to burn as his heart thumped and almost broke out of his rib cage. Gradually he was losing consciousness but he knew if he just gave up he would die in that cold, strange place and no one would even know where he was. Every now and then the thought of Monty being in his ear made him continue to survive even when he felt there was no energy left to try with. He kept on swimming for what seemed to be hours, and then suddenly he found he was at the surface and now able to breathe a lot better. But there was something which was so close to his head, which was preventing him from coming out of the water properly.

Hardly able to move by now, he began to crawl around on rocks that rose up out of this stormy place and bit by bit he was beginning to feel solid ground underneath his feet. The air was different here and there was a strange light just ahead of him. Finally he opened his eyes fully and looked for a long time in all directions to see if could recognise where he was or make any sense of the unusual surrounds. By this time Monty had regained consciousness, and began to squeak and squeal again, as he slowly chewed away the hair that he had become entangled in Lions' ear. Lion was annoyed at the frequent tugging of the hairs as they were being ripped away by Monty's frequent attempts for freedom.

Eventually he was free from what had initially had him trapped. Yet it was at the same time he perceived that it was definitely something of safety that had kept him close to Lion. Slowly he began to peep out from inside Lions ear.

This is a truly strange place Lion, where on earth are we, do you know?

Lion did not answer at first; after all he was still trying to breathe properly which was still quite difficult because he had held his breath for so long that he was now barely conscious.

Slowly he started to follow the strong instinct which drew him closer and closer to the light.

Fear of being in a strange place could no longer hold him still. The closer he came to the lighted area the stronger his breathing became, the clearer he could see again and excitement began to stir again within his majestic heart.

Come on Monty, come on, hop up on my back again and let's go and see what that light is just up ahead.

Oh Lion Monty squeaked, are you sure we are not going to be eaten by some large creature which not even you can protect us from?

Is this that strange place called heaven that we hear humans talking about at times, where you are supposed to walk into the light or some such crazy thing?

I do not know and no longer care what is there up ahead of us Monty, All I do know is that we should be there, so come on let's just get there and find out for ourselves.

It was not long before Lion could feel a much smoother level of ground under his feet, his steps became surer and quicker as he looked down to see what was underneath him. He was surprised to see how white the sand was under his paws and the warmth of it between his toes.

Look Monty, how strangely white and beautiful that sand is. See how it seems to sparkle like a million stars in the night time out in the bush.

Monty quickly slid down the side of Lion and wanted to try out this beautiful shiny stuff for himself which was under Lions paws.

Lion, Lion, It moves around so much between my paws, and see, look at this shiny gold stuff which seems to be sticking to my toes.

Lion finally just sat down, unable to move any further because of his deep exhaustion.

It wasn't long before Monty came back and snuggled down between Lions paws. Soon they both fell asleep, awaking later not knowing how long they had slept, and a little frightened not knowing where they were.

I am so hungry Lion. I can't remember when we ate last time.

Actually Monty, so am I. Yawning and carefully stretching all his muscles so he could get his body working again Lion slowly stood and looked around to see where he may be able to get something to eat.

The first thing he noticed was how close to his head the ground above him seemed to be.

Lion, I don't understand. Why is the ground above our heads? I thought we were supposed to walk on the ground while it stayed under out feet.

Little by little as they both timidly investigated their strange, cold and wet surroundings, they realised that they were in fact in some kind of a cave with a very low ceiling. The roof was not far from the top of the water. However, where they stood the ground spread out and gently sloped downwards, the closer they moved nearer to the light.

Eventually they came to realise that much of the beautiful light that surrounded them, was indeed coming from the thousands of tiny little fire flies which buzzed around while many others just clung to the walls which surrounded them.

Lion became inquisitive and quietly investigated the tiny lights which moved themselves around so freely. Some of them landed gently on his nose. The tiny things tickled as they quietly flicked here and there. Lion was shocked at how light they were, how small they were and how quickly they moved from place to place. But there was still another strange, pale blue green light coming from up ahead. Lion and Monty began moving a little quicker towards the light and had almost forgotten how sore and tired they were when they first came to this place in the cold and darkness of the night before.

Both of them had begun to sniff the air and wonder what that the strange smell was, because somehow it seemed familiar to them.

Lion, something is familiar about that smell, do you think there is something we have smelt like that before? I seem to remember that we may have even had something disgusting to eat which smelt a bit like that. Suddenly they both realised, with many other things now flooding back to their conscious memory. They had indeed eaten many tiny smelly things which someone had brought to them a long time ago.

Oh Lion, I just realised that someone is missing. Where do you think Eagle has gone to? Doesn't he care how we are, has she gone off and left us alone, lost in this strange place with no one to tell us where to go or how to get some food?

Does she expect us to actually go out and hunt for food by ourselves?

I would not know what is safe for us to eat. And by the way, what are we going to drink? I cannot see any nice clear water anywhere here.

Lion had gradually come to where the light was shining the brightest, and saw that the water was moving gently off to the right hand side. He felt a gentle, warm breeze moving into the cave, and saw many golden butterflies flying just above the water. The ceiling became much higher there, the walls shone like liquid copper, and hundreds of deep golden, purple and vivid blue butterflies hovered above attracted by the sparkling water. They had been coming early every morning to that place of beautiful water for hundreds of years. Monty was now standing in awe at such a beautiful sight.

The butterflies looked like sparkling jewels to him, yet at the same time another memory was surfacing more clearly to his mind which brought a deep sense of sadness and silence.

Monty, why are so quiet all of a sudden? Oh, I was just remembering my beautiful Priscilla and how much I miss her he responded with tears rolling down his little cheeks.

Then all the butterflies turned in one movement, like a ripple in the water, and came rushing closer to where Lion and Monty stood. Their movement seemed to be carrying a strange and wonderful music with them.

Monty thought he could hear whispered words, but said nothing just in case he sounded strange to his mighty friend Lion.

The butterflies circled above their heads with the sway of the wonderful music continuing and tiny flashes of light reflecting and flashing everywhere off their wings.

Lion could no longer stay quiet and whispered to Monty if he thought he could hear any of the sounds which seemed to be like whispered words.

As they stood there smiling at each other, the words became clearer.

Excuse me, excuse me, did you say Priscilla?

Monty twisted his little head around as he asked who is speaking Lion?Then the largest of all the butterflies came and rested gently, right on the middle of Lions nose. Her beautiful iridescent wings seemed to have colours which rapidly changed and sparkled like a diamond, every time she made the slightest move.

Tears ran down Monty's face as he realised someone else knew his beautiful Priscilla. Yes he responded with joy. I knew a beautiful butterfly named Priscilla. When I was asleep in the jungle one day, there was large snake silently slithering towards me, ready to eat me I believe. Priscilla had softly awoken me as she brushed the tips of her lovely wings against my nose and spoke just like you are now. She saved my life but then went away just as the rain began to fall.

Mouse, the butterfly whispered, Priscilla butterfly was the queen and our leader. All these beautiful creatures here around us are from the one tribe called La Mariposa. Priscilla who is also my mother said that many years ago after the first breeding time of the year there came a terrible storm to the original country of our tribe.

Where is that country, is it very far away? Monty squeaked.

Oh yes little one it is many, many miles away, and normally we could never have come this far except for the powerful winds which carried my mother and all her family.

What is your name asked Lion, and what is the name of that far away place.

Oh I am sorry, I should have introduced myself before now the pretty one said. My name is El angel, which means angel or messenger.

The country where the history of my family was first known about is called Rodavlas.

Then another darker coloured and much larger butterfly came close to lion and mouse and began to speak in the same strange musical words, as she fluttered close by but with a sound of authority.

My name is Florita, which means flower; I am called that because I am able to find the best flowers for drinking nectar far quicker than most other Mariposa. I am Priscilla's older sister. I was blown over to this strange place at the end of the same storm which carried her here.

I have been wondering where my sister went to a few days ago.

She heard someone strange calling her and she went to investigate what was happening, but she never came back to tell us about it. To us all sounds are like music. Some music is pleasant to listen to and some definitely hurts our ears and we will often move as far away as possible from that place. Just yesterday as I was looking for some fresh nectar I saw those precious wings of my sister stuck on a thorn. The flashing blue light from them caught my attention because though her body wasn't there they were scattered in small pieces on the nearby branches. They shone in the sun light like little pearly treasures. Priscilla had markings like eyes among the other dull brown distinct markings underneath her wings which no one else has, and they were still sparkling like precious Jewells. The voice was quite distressed which drew her attention, so she went to share whatever comfort or encouragement that she could.

My sister has always been a very good teacher and has always been able to teach others how to survive in strange places and dangerous situations.

Her daughter El angel has those same qualities too. In fact it was the sound of mouses calling which drew her towards you, she wants to teach you mouse about the strength you have inside you which you haven't even begun to use yet. She wants to show you how to be confident when your friends just disappear from your sight.

What is your name any way mouse? I am Monty. Florita, why were Priscilla's wings all in little pieces?

Well, some birds love to eat butterflies, but they mostly eat our bodies and leave the wings behind. There is a lot of fat and nutrients in our bodies which is like medicine to them. At least because her beautiful wings were left behind, I can remember how beautiful she was as she soared in the air high above me. Because of that special memory I can after a while stop hurting for her loss and be content to know her spirit has gone to a far better place than in these jungles.

Well Monty, I would love to share with you some ideas how you can help yourself to be bold and courageous next time you feel as though no one else is there to help and protect you.

Wait just a moment Florita said, I think we should at least have something to drink before we do anything else. I shall go and see where the best flowers are so we can have something sweet to drink.

I will go and look for some food for you Lion said, you must be very hungry now after all the tossing and turning in the water last night. I won't be long, so don't you start worrying again little one lion softly spoke to Monty. He then began to tentatively move around below that low ceiling. Florita said he would be better off if he followed her out into the new part of the jungle. You see Monty you have been washed off the large island you had been on and on to a much smaller one. It is beautiful here but unless you know where you are going you can still come to serious harm or even be permanently lost. Lion followed immediately but could not keep up with Floritas swift flight.

Still he determined to keep going now that he had started, and he certainly didn't want his little friend to go hungry any longer. Everything was so strangely beautiful here and totally unfamiliar. He did not see which direction Florita had gone and in fact went in the opposite direction to her. It wasn't long before he became quite lost but this time not afraid. He looked everywhere all the time wondering what he could actually eat and what would be appropriate to take back to Monty.

He continued to wander around not having any idea where he was and still tired from his horrendous journey from the night before. Many times he lay down under some bush or tree in the cool shade and had what he thought was just a short sleep. Each time he rested he thought he could smell some beautiful but strange perfume but didn't know where it was coming from. Each time he fell asleep he thought he could hear a strange music that carried unusual words, but again didn't know where any of the wonder was coming from. After a while he lost all sense of pain and weariness but also the fact he had a small friend waiting for him.

This went on for many hours.

With barely a movement Florita was airborne and had moved swiftly through the bright green light and out into the jungle just beyond the mouth of the cave they were in, off to another part of the nearby jungle. As she drew nearer an unusually strong perfume drew her into its midst. For a short time she was unable to navigate to any specific flower to gather some nectar. As she flew slowly through the flowers a gentle breeze began to lift her up and down as if huge arms were carrying her. A sound as that of many gentle winds drifted throughout the whole area. Florita felt perhaps they were singing but couldn't clearly make out any of the words.

She was intoxicated by the sounds and the sweet perfume and landed on the edge of the largest orchid she had seen or imagined.

The pale mauve petals with the deep purple throat softly moved across her wings and she was instantly refreshed by their touch and the liquid they left on her. She was amazed as she took her time and looked around her. Many Huge flowers were growing on the sides of most of the trees, adorning them with their soft and sometimes brilliant beauty. The soft breeze continued in that area of paradise and created the amazing effects of smell, sight and touch which for a time caused Florita to forget the beauty, sight and sound of any other place.

As the breeze stopped each flower turned their heads towards her. The large purple orchids seemed to be smiling at her as they bent their head and dripped their abundant scent all over her. It was strange she thought that this moisture was not actually making her become weighed down.

Splashes of bright yellow flowers twisted and turned like miniature ballerinas. Sky Blue flowers appeared to be clapping their hands in tune to the movements of the yellow flowers.

Large, bright red lilies stood serenely as they overlooked the activities in front of them. Purple lilies grew throughout the field of this floral paradise. There were so many flowers growing there that there wasn't much room for any grass to grow.

Florita began to wonder why there were no other insects little animals or birds of any kind amongst them. She uttered the words to the wind and the wind responded this way;

OH GENTLE LADY WITH WINGS SO BLUE
WE ARE HERE FOR THE SAKE OF YOU
NO MAN COMES OR BEAUTIFUL BIRD
NO INSECT SOUNDS THAT CAN BE HEARD

BUT ON OCCASSIONS WHICH ARE UNSEEN
ANOTHER COMES AS IF IN A DREAM
HIS GARMENTS GLOW BOTH WHITE AND GOLD
AND HIS VOICE OF LOVE CAN NOT BE TOLD

I TELL YOU NOW OF THIS IM SURE
HIS PRESENCE BRINGS AN OPEN DOOR
SOME COME IN AND SOME WILL NOT
TO US HE WILL NOT SOON BE FORGOT

Oh beloved wind Florita cried, can I bring others here too. Only, the wind replied if they can be quiet and listen to the wind, smell the many perfumes here and watch the dance of the flowers without wanting to roughly pick them and take them home with them. They will never be able to take pictures of them nor take any roots or cuttings with the idea of growing them elsewhere. This little patch of paradise is for the gentle and pure of heart to enter here but only for fleeting moments at a time. Only if they are looking for the best of what they can give to others to quench their thirst, will they be able to find, see or enter this place. So dear Florita, think carefully and listen carefully to what your heart tells you if you ever attempt to bring anyone here. Be careful, for if you act unwisely with your new information you too will never be able to find this place again.

I shall be careful wind, but why would I never be able to find my way here again. Because beautiful one, if you stop listening to the quietness of your heart and what secrets it gives you, you will not see clearly and your sense of direction will not be straight. If there is any harsh noise the flowers here will fold up and sleep till the ugly sounds disappear.

It is the sounds in the quietness which the flowers respond to and come out to dance or greet whoever comes to this place. Most humans will never find this place because they will always want to analyse, control or at least rearrange what has been perfect and beautiful for a very long time. The sound of their own heart beat is too fast and too loud for them to hear what you have heard this day. The perfumes here are so rare they would be counted as garbage by most; they are smells most have never experienced before. The sights of the dancing flowers would only ever be counted as forced movement because of an assumed wind. But beautiful one, you have seen for yourself how they dance and have heard them singing. You have seen the light emanating from the lighter coloured ones. You have seen the way the blue ones knew how to keep time with the golden ones as they danced to an unheard orchestra. You have seen the actual joy on the faces of all these flowers, don't forget it, but just be very careful what you share with anyone of what you have seen and heard here. The tall flowers that are hidden in this secluded area never die, but they still have to receive tender love and care and protection from the one who visits silently but very often. Now go beautiful one, and I would suggest you look in the next little secluded area of trees over there and you will see a little stream where you can take your friends to quench their thirst. But even there please ask them to be gentle to the plants and not to pick or cut any of them.

Florita thought perhaps she should first check out the new place before she took any one there. As she entered the new area she was amazed at the multitude of different colours of flashing lights. They were all so tiny and yet light up the whole section of the jungle. She stood quietly on a small rock near the edge of the water and tried to see what was causing the lights to dance all around her.

As she looked closer and stilled the excitement in her heart she noticed that the lights were coming from the centre of many different kinds of flowers. Not knowing how long she had stood there she had also lost track of the time and it had now become night. As the sun set behind the mountains near by it became much cooler and darker quite suddenly in that special place. With all the changes which were happening Florita did not consider for a moment to fly back to her friends. She remained almost entranced with the beauty of these surrounds. The light from the gems in the centres of the flowers now made them appear transparent. As they swayed in the cool evening breeze many hundreds of butterflies gathered around them and Florita was delighted to see how many different colours there were amongst them. No two butterflies were the same either in their colouring or their markings. Who are you she stammered? We are the ones who gather nectar of a night time to fill the cup that someone places each night at the edge of the jungle. We heard someone whisper a long time ago asking us for something sweet to drink. At the time we were quite frightened at the deep sound of that strange voice. After a long time we investigated where it came from, and found that it belonged to one who is like a man but much quieter and gentler than other humans we had seen outside the jungle. We asked why it was to be us to gather the nectar and the stranger told us no one else had ever stopped and investigated the source of the voice. He told us where to look and we quickly discovered that as we all gathered in unity for the filling of the cup we too were being refreshed by the same nectar. Many generations of our different families have been taught of the beauty and trained to fill that cup. Each one of us does not live long and we need to start training them as soon as they have learnt how to fly. We always have gathered only from that pure sweet water in the stream near the rock where you are standing and nowhere else, and we only ever gather of a night time. Many humans come here and sit amongst the flowers for a time. Some have been here as the gems begin to light up this area and they have stolen the heart of the flowers just for the sake of a presumed wealth they could gain. They have all discovered that once the gems leave this area they appear to turn into normal stones without any value to those that try to put a price on them. Most of those humans have become quite ill because of the strange happenings with their gems. They become angry and spiteful when they realise they have made a huge mistake in taking the gems for themselves and then they cannot receive any gain from them.

Suddenly all the butterflies lift up with droplets of sweet water still clinging to their tiny legs. We shall see you some other time if you are still here they sang, and suddenly they had all disappeared. Florita then remembered why she was there and flew off to where her friends had been waiting.

To her it seemed a long time since she left her friends behind so she could look for water, but as she alighted on a small rock near mouse they greeted her in surprise. They seriously doubted that her short time away was long enough to find anything beneficial for them.

Florita explained only the second place that she had found and pleaded with them not to take any of the gems or break any of the flowers as they enjoyed the new place and refreshed themselves at the stream of sweet water.

When she arrived back at the entrance of the cave which appeared from the outside to be mostly under water, she saw eagle standing there and smiled at him. Why don't you go inside Florita asked? I cannot fly through the entrance so I shall stand here and talk to Monty and the others as they stay sheltered under the rock ceiling. They will come out soon enough. Then hopefully they will be ready to hear the further directions I have for them to get off this smaller island and back onto the main island.

Where is lion, he did not follow me. I shall go now eagle said and tell him to come back. Eagle lifted her mighty wings and was instantly airborne with one or two flaps of them. When she found lion wandering around in another part of the jungle he called to him to follow. This time Lion was ready to listen and followed without any further trouble.

Now lion was reminded of the friendship which had been building over the last many months as he travelled with Monty and eagle. Oh dear, oh dear he rumbled, where is my little friend, is he alright, is he very hungry I had forgotten all about him in this beautiful place?

Lion, settle down he is alright. I know you wanted to the best thing for him, but you have to remember that you too sometimes need rest.

Because of your exhaustion from the journey through the turbulent waters you had become exhausted and as you entered this beautiful place you began to relax and your mind closed down for a short time, other than the fact that you felt safe here. But do not worry, mouse is quite safe he has remained with all the beautiful butterflies and has been drinking from the sweet water in the cave under the rock at the edge of the ocean. Lion followed the callings of eagle but at the same time had not been carefully watching where he had been placing his big paws with each step. Oh Lion, Lion please be careful there, you must stop and I will show you what you nearly did. Lion was puzzled but stopped still on the spot. Eagle landed right beside him. Bend down and see what you nearly fell through Lion. As eagle moved aside some of the rambling vines below lions paws and told him to look down, Lion gasped with shock. He could clearly see that it was a long way down to the deep waters of the dark ocean. Thank you eagle, I am so glad I didn't have to go through another journey through such strong waters again, and then stepped aside into the solid path just a few inches off to the side. Soon after that they arrived safely at the cave entrance. Eagle flew to the top of a lone pine tree and settled down for the night. I will see you and talk to you and Monty in the morning Lion, now go and have a good rest you will need the strength. Lion bent down and quietly went in to the others that waited for his return.

Because it was totally dark now, they all decided to wait till the next morning and then go for the beautiful water. Everyone including the butterflies, who were the friends and family of Florita, settled down for a good night's rest.

Early next morning they were awaken by a strong and strange smell. A strong wind was beginning to blow all around them and Monty began to be afraid. Where is lion, where is lion he squeaked and turned his little head to see lion right beside him smiling at him? Where is eagle where is eagle, Monty squeaked again? I am here right above you in the tall tree which you slept against all night. Mouse looked up and fell over backwards as he leant backwards trying to focus on eagle.

Lion began to enquire as to where he would be able to find some food to fill his rumbling stomach.

They had begun to walk off to the new place that eagle was describing to them. The wind became angrier and the smell got stronger all the time. Mouse scurried off in the wrong direction and Lion pursued close behind to bring him back to safety and suddenly they both stopped dead in their tracks for they had found a long line of the same smelly things which eagle had brought to them before.

They were both now hungry enough to start eating them without grumbling or complaining. In fact mouse surprised himself and ate so many of the smelly things that his belly was dragging on the ground. He stopped and lay down to rest for a while and discovered many of the strange hard things that had come from the smelly fish things. Without thinking lion and he had just spat them out as they ate. Now he remembered how eagle had told them to gather many of the same things and put them in a little bag under the fur on their necks. At the same time he and lion began to look for that little bag and quickly discovered it was indeed still there. They again began to gather as many of the hard things as they could and were surprised to see how easily the bag continued to grow as they put each one in. They gathered every one of those hard things that they could see and still the bag around their neck was no heavier.

Where do you think the smelly things have come from Lion? As lion was about to offer some explanation Eagle came and stood beside them and said, there was a tsunami last night which caused everything at the bottom of the ocean to be washed ashore to where you now see them. Because of where you stayed to sleep was so protected and special you were not even touched by it.

But come on now we must keep moving there is a larger storm coming over the end of the jungle. You will have enough time to have a drink at the special stream and then we must go to the other side of the island to stay safe.

The rest of the butterflies caught up to them and implored them to hurry which they did do. Mouse and lion were only allowed to visit the special place because there would be no room for them to stay any length of time once the flowers began to go back to their survival mode.

All entered the special area and all had a long drink from the beautiful sweet water. Then Florita explained to mouse and lion that they should leave because the flowers were going to start to fold up and wrap themselves around the trees as they entwined themselves around each other so as not to be washed away when the tsunami hit.

Mouse and lion did not get the chance to see the gems light up in the heart of the flowers but they still wanted to help if they could. No Florita said when the flowers begin to close down they can no longer see or hear anything except the strange voice which keeps on whispering just trust me, just rust me until the tsunami is over and they can begin to unfold again.

Lion and Monty again remember the small sack tied to their neck, hidden in the hair on their chest

They felt they should gather many more of the hard things, and put them in the sack because somehow they also felt they would not be coming back this way again. They wanted to take as much as possible which seemed to be of value to eagle, though they didn't know why. No, no eagle screamed, you no longer have any time left let's go now. All the butterflies lifted together and sang their good byes as they disappeared higher into the trees of the nearby jungle.

Again Monty and Lion began to run like they had so long ago just after they had met. Again they didn't really know where they were headed but decided to trust eagle and at least try to listen carefully to the directions she gave. Please Lion, I can no longer keep up with your large steps can I please hop onto your back again so I don't get left behind and lost? Oh sure, come on Monty I am so sorry I didn't think of it earlier. Once more Monty dug his little paws into the hair in Lions' main and hung on for dear life.

Every now and then eagle would disappear above the dark clouds that had swiftly developed above the jungle canopy. But she was back with her two companions just as swiftly each time. You must hurry lion the storm is almost upon you. You are almost at the base of a large mountain; unless you get there before the storm does you will be washed away again.

Lion and Monty were surprised to hear eagle talk about mountains in this beautiful place. Lion began to think negatively about the possible hike up the mountain. But this time he kept his thoughts to himself for he did not want to alarm Monty any further.

Monty fell asleep and awoke full of courage and wanted to try for himself what it was like to race against the oncoming storm. Stop, stop he cried to lion, which he did do. Monty slid to the ground and began to run in all directions attempting to make himself look big and important. Before he knew what was happening he had slid off the side of the track and indeed off the side of the mountain which they had just began to climb.

Eagle keen eye caught sight of mouses fall and swiftly swooped low and scooped him up and put him back on the track where he would be safe again. That's not fair eagle, why can't I go where the big paws of Lion go? Monty, do you remember how Priscilla told you that you were made exactly the way you were meant to be. Well your tiny feet cannot go where the large paws of lion are meant to go. Plus his feet are padded differently and that's why he doesn't slip and slide around on the wet ground as much as yours do.

Do you remember how you used to hide in the cracks of the floors long ago; well you see Lion would never be able to put his large paws in those small places at all. Monty was comforted to think he had some specific reason for tiny paws and settled again on Lions back. They were soon on their way again as the storm developed into a noisy harassing animal. Red sheet Lightening began to flash across the sky as jagged bolts of white hot lightening began to crack so close to them on the ground. The thunder cracked and shook the ground underneath them and lion s paws took on a speed which surprised even him. Mouse didn't wait to be told to go to safety in lions ears; he simply scurried there without hesitation.

Eagle, eagle I can smell smoke what's happening? There is a large raging fire which has started in the valley where you have just come from and the wind is driving it up the mountain. Hurry Lion, hurry or you will be burnt to death. Lion continued on as the sparks of the pursuing fire began to land near him in the bushes. The bushes began to explode into fire balls. Many parts of lion's fur began to burn from the sparks which landed in his mane. Don't stop don't stop lion you are nearly at the top now. By then Lion and Monty could both hear the roar of the fire behind and all around them. Lion was finding it hard to breathe properly but continued on. His paws' began to burn from the fire which was now crossing their track, still he kept going.

Then quite suddenly the wind changed its direction and the fire began to burn back on itself. Not long after that they were at the top and lion sat down on the only piece of rock that did not seem to have been burnt. The coolness of it certainly helped him to cool down and rest. Eagle landed on the rock beside him. Lion have a look out over the valley below you, and you will see just how far you have come carrying Monty on your back. Lion looked out over the valley as eagle asked and saw many other mountains off in the distance. Most of the valleys had been burn out by the raging fire. There was one valley however that seemed to be free from fire damage. It seemed to whisper to come closer with its lush green vegetation barely visible from where they now sat. The mountain which was closest to them was black like death. Everything on it had been burnt earlier during the fire storm. All that could be seen now was the dying embers and smoke as it filled the lower valleys.

Do not worry Lion, I will go and get some plants which will help you heal from your burns. Eagle way soon out of sight and out over another mountain range. Monty stayed a long time in Lions ear and did not come out till eagle returned with a strange looking cactus in his beak. Monty, I want you to use your strong little paws and chew this till its juices come out. Then I want you to put it all over lion's burns please. Ok eagle I know I can do that for you. Lion and Monty spent many days on the mountain top as eagle brought them many more of the same smelly things to eat and many times with his beak filled with water to put in the shells of the smelly things for them to drink.

When eagle could see that Lion was fully recovered and ready to move on he stirred them one morning when there before them was a glorious sunrise which filled them all with joy to see. Come on, time to make some real progress through the rest of the valleys' and mountain ranges before we all get home again. That night, totally exhausted lion asked how far they had come. Surely he moaned we have come such a long way, I feel as though we have anyway. Well eagle said as you sit on this new mountain which you climbed today have a look around you and tell me what you see. Lion was shocked to see that they had only come across to one mountain and it was the one which was so badly burnt. He hadn't taken much notice how they had travelled through the ashes of the fire, or how there were no longer trees or bushes left that they could rest under. Sometimes Lion we think we have come a long way on our journey, but that's only because of the struggles we went through on the way. But still that is one less mountain you will have to climb over later isn't it. You have learnt many valuable things today lion and tomorrow you will understand how to appreciate them much better than I can explain to you today. Now rest and I will go and get some food and drink for you.

Soon eagle returned, again with the same smelly things. Disappearing many times to come back with his beak filled with sweet water for them to drink from the shells.

Early the next morning they were awoken by a cool refreshing breeze. Their energy returned and they quickly set off to the next valley or mountain as eagle gave them clear directions. Lion was surprised at how strong he now felt; after all I have only been eating those smelly things and haven't had any meat for such a long time he uttered.

He began to think for the first time in many months what it would be like to finally be in his own home land and he had totally lost track of how far and how fast he was travelling. That night there was the same procedure of eagle bringing back the smelly things and the beak full of water many times, for their nourishment.

As the sun set with its rays of gold and liquid rubies eagle asked Lion to look out over the valley and see what he could see. Lion saw a lush green valley which seemed only a short way away. It looks so familiar he rumbled. It should be lion that is your home land we should be there by tomorrow evening. This time he saw that they had come over many mountain ranges and through many valleys and all in that one day.

What has been the difference he asked eagle? Lion for once you did not doubt or fear. You trusted the directions I gave and you followed them exactly and therefore you were able to work and come much further than you have ever believed possible before.

Again there was the same procedure of the smelly things and the beaks full of water. They settled down much quicker this night with strange and unusual peace filling them. Just before dark fully settled over them a gentle rain began to fall and lion was a little frightened to see a large silhouette of a golden lions head glistening just off to the right above them. There was an eagle which appeared to be made of liquid gold flying between the lions' head and the eagle friend which had accompanied them for so long. The conversation between the three of them was not understood by Monty or lion, but this time they felt not to ask any questions.

Lion fell asleep with mouse resting on his big paw. The golden lion in the clouds watched them closely and smiled for he knew what was ahead of them the next morning. But he also knew they would not have been ready to go back home earlier, nor would they have learnt any of the valuable lessons of life if they had not gone through the pain and troubles of mountain climbing, racing through fires and struggling through the raging waters.

Early the next morning again with the warmth and beauty of another glorious sunrise Monty awoke delighted with the soft pillow under his head, and ran up and down outside lion's nose till he too woke up.

Come now my beautiful companions, it is time to travel one shorter journey. Eagle stood there beside them but Lion noticed he had tears in his eyes. What is the matter eagle he asked? Oh I am alright really; it's just that I know our journey together is almost finished and it makes me a little sad. After today I shall never see you again. But if you call out to the golden eagle in the sky he will hear you and will always be ready to come and listen if you want to talk or come and give you the help and directions no one else can. He is able to show you far more than I ever could in many life times. He will show you many wonders of the hidden valleys and secluded places of rare beauty. But you will need to be quiet to be able to hear him, for he always talks much softer than I ever could. Just be ready and expect to hear from him any time day or night, but remember, he cannot talk to anybody who will not listen carefully and take the full time that is needed to really hear what is being said.

Eagle, Monty squeaked, won't you please tell me about these hard things we have been gathering for so long, and why they all fitted in the bag which was so small at the beginning.

Oh Monty, I was hoping you or lion would ask me some day about them.

If you remember each one of them came from inside the flesh of the smelly things which are called oysters. If a grain of sand or any other foreign object gets into the flesh of oysters, it causes great pain to it. The oyster becomes quite agitated in its attempts to be rid of it. It spins a special substance around the irritant and that settles in a hard and shiny surface all around it. That substance is called nacre.

Well o.k. eagle but why was it so important for us to gather so many, and how come they all fitted to the one little bag Lion and I have been carrying around our necks.

Monty, you will see if you look closely that the bags around your necks are actually a part of your own body. Have a look and see what shape they are. Monty and lion both looked at their bags around their necks and then checked out each others to see if they were the same kind of thing.

They were both amazed at how beautiful the others bag was and the shape was a puzzle to them. Lion vaguely remembered seeing something like this somewhere before but could not remember what it was called. Eagle watched the puzzlement on both their faces and gently explained that it was their hearts that they had been looking at. Also eagle explained that each time they made room in their hearts by faith to place the hard things there the more their hearts grew. Because it had been a natural progression of what they put in there, it was not a heavy burden for them to carry.

Yes but, why the great importance of gathering them Monty interrupted, of what good are they?

Monty, there are some people on the main land that love to gather them and sometimes make jewellery out of them. Sometimes people gather them simply for the value of them. The smoother they are and the shiner they are the more money they are worth. You and Lion are not used to dealing with money and really you have no need for it either. But if you have a look at the people on the main land, especially at Malkendah you may wish to share some of the precious things with them. You may want just to encourage them that they are allowed to have some beautiful things. Or you may want to give them to the ladies in the castle at the lower end of the road where I used to live, to sell and use for the villagers needs. That will be up to you though. You may even want to keep some for yourself to remind yourselves of the incredible journey you have taken together. But Eagle, we are animals, so how can we talk to the humans and make ourselves clearly understood. I have learnt to hear sometimes what horse was saying each time I left the gateway eagle said. I am confident and believe by now the ladies living in the castle have learnt to understand what horse is saying at least to some degree. So little one just take them to the horse and he will give them to the ladies and explain what they are for. If you go there early in the morning as the sun rises you will not be scared away by all the inquisitive people and their attempts at stopping you from entering their village. They do that sort of thing because they have been through many hard times and they are simply trying to protect themselves.

After you have been to the castle even once you will really love it and all the special things that happen there especially of a night time. There is plenty of room for you both to live the rest of your lives out the back of the castle. There you will find plenty of the normal foods which you are both used to and you will never again have to hunt in the same way as you have had to recently. But you must go there for yourselves; no one else can really make you enjoy all the beautiful things that happen. You must find out though and experience it all for yourselves.

Monty, if you had never eaten any of the smelly and distasteful things then you would have never found any of the hard things called pearls either. Oh, I see now he squeaked. I am so glad then that you were patient enough to continually encourage us to gather them.

Eagle flew off to the last valley in front of her, but continued calling Monty and mouse to keep going and keep climbing a little higher with each step they took.

Finally eagle landed in the top of the same tree where Sarsha fell through so long ago. Lion and Monty sat in the cool shade at the foot of that huge tree and began to work out if they go to the main land which was above the tree or whether they would stay here in a place which was seemingly normal to them. After all Monty squeaked there are no humans here are there. No Lion rumbled but then what would we do with these pearls? Oh well, if you are game Lion I guess I can go with you too to talk to horse and give him the pearls for the women. I guess it would also be good to check out what it is going to be like in our new home behind the castle, after all I don't really want to be left on my own again.

Sarsha, Sarsha where are you Manuel called gently?

Who is that Lion and Monty asked spontaneously?

Eagle began to carefully edge her way down the branches towards the level of the big rocks. I am here Manuel I won't be long; it's a bit awkward trying to hang on with just two big feet and claws.

Sarsha had begun to waver in her ability to go between being a quiet, unassuming woman and a mighty eagle. Monty and Lion watched and listened very carefully to everything that was being said, they had never seen or heard anything like this before.

As Sarsha came closer to the level of rocks she changed back to her human form and suddenly realised she had on the same beautiful gown that Manuel had made and given her in his shop many months before.

She stepped down on to the rock and stood smiling at Manuel. He was surrounded by the beautiful rays of morning sunshine and stood in greater appearance of powerful, majestic beauty than Sarsha had previously seen or noticed.

Oh Nivek, lion, you are here too how wonderful to see all of you again. I have missed you so much while I was away for so long. Oh, but you have only been away for a few moments Manuel commented. This is the same morning and the same sunrise as when you first flew down from the top of that tree.

Now Dear Sarsha I want you to go back down there just once more. I am so tired she cried cant it wait a little longer.

No dear one this is the right time for you.

Alright then, but why do you want me to go down there again it was a hard time down there for me and I don't think I can do much at this point.

Dear Sarsha you have left the exact amount of love and energy that is required for the simple task.

I want you to go to the island where Lion and Monty were washed up into that underground place with the low ceiling. Yes, but why Manuel?

I want you to stand at the edge of the entrance and look closely at the vines and shrubs on the ground just away from the cave entrance. As you do so you will see the ocean beneath it stand quite still as the waves rise up; and stand still in mid air as they hang there. I want you to go to the bottom of that particular ocean spot and pick up that large black pearl which has lain there for many, many years.

It is yours but you must be the one to go and gather it up. But Manuel I will be drowned if I go there and all the waves of the ocean fall on top of me. You know it is not natural for eagles to be covered by water. My feathers will become water logged and I will not be able to fly. I shall be killed and buried forever in a watery grave.

Just this one last thing Sarsha and remember the words you heard long ago, just rust me, just trust.

Once more a strange peace settled over Sarsha and she instantly decided to go and get it all over and done with. She stepped back on to the tree where her legs became again as those of a mighty eagle with large talons at the end of them, and climbed to the top of it.

The lion at the bottom of the tree and the lion at the top of the rocks where Nivek and Manuel stood both roared in delight. Sarsha stepped off and flew down to the place she had just come from. Down and down she swiftly flew like a spiralling spear. It was only moment later as she landed at the cave entrance. She took her time to scratch away some of the vines to find what Manuel spoke of and saw such a long way down exactly what he explained. She hesitated for a few seconds thinking of how many times she had told lion and Monty to gather the pearls for the bag around their neck. It looks like it is my time to take the same good action and just see what comes of it.

She pulled aside quite a large patch of the entangled vines and dove down to the bottom of that part of the ocean, trusting that the huge waves would not collapse over the top of her. And there she gathered the large black pearl in her beak. As she flew back to the entrance of the cave she was amazed at how big the pearl was. It looked so tiny from where she first looked down to it, but now she could hardly hold it in her huge beak.

She stood still for only a few moments then flew back to the tree where Manuel and Nivek waited for her.

Sarsha found it quite difficult to continue holding the large pearl in her beak, she wanted to cry out for help but the desire not to lose the pearl was stronger so she rested for a while in the tree, then steadily inched her way down through the branches back again to the level of the top of the rocks where they were waiting for her. She stood just below the ridge of the rocks and placed the black pearl on the rock just above her head, and it was in those faltering moments that she lost all her confidence to fly again like a mighty eagle. Come on said Manuel I will help you up the last few steps. As Sarsha put one hand up for Manuel she stretched the other out to take up the black pearl but found something else was in the same place.

Sarsha Has One More Chance

Manuel drew her up to the top of the rock and said now bend down and take up the pearl. She bent down to do so and saw a small baby lying on the only patch of green grass right beside the pearl.

What is that doing there Manuel and who is it. What is that strange piece of material beside it, which looks exactly like the material in the first dress you made and gave me? Oh look, I see that that is the one on me now.

Manuel spoke softer than he had at other times, Sarsha that little girl is one of those which Nivek has been trying to look after out the back of your castle. He has tried many times to get you to help him but was unable to get your full attention. He was waiting at the bottom of the stairs which we had just descended the night before you went to the new lands far away. I have explained to him that you have tried many times to help save many babies of those you picked up as you went through the war torn places and other areas of turmoil. You had lost heart and closed off your emotions and efforts to help when so many of them died. I know you no longer wanted to be discouraged or hurt with any further losses of their precious lives.

Sarsha I want you to have this one chance of seeing a precious baby girl living after you have helped them. I would like you to pick up the baby and wrap it in that beautiful material beside it, then just hand her to me. I will take her to my work shop for a while and then one day when she is ready I will take her to the women in the castle. After she has learnt many beautiful things about love and life I will then my father's castle on the mountain. Do you remember the bundle you saw under my arm when you met me here on the rocks, well this is the little one that I was holding then.

Sarsha bent down with the last bit of energy she had left and gathered the little one in her arms and gently wrapped it in the lovely, glowing white cloth which Manuel had bought with him. She sobbed deeply as her tears fell upon the little ones face making it glow like a beautiful pearl. Then she gently handed the precious little girl to Manuel.

I am tired Manuel can we all sit together over on that rock where I used to sit as I overlooked the valley below. They all gathered on the rock and Sarsha was surprised to see all the gems off the second wet dress which had been ruined in the rain long ago were sitting in a shallow pool of water just behind them.

She placed her pearl in with them just to see how they looked together and wondered at the perfect unity of their togetherness.

What shall I do with the pearl Manuel she asked? That is up to you Sarsha but you may want to consider using it for the help of all the babies Nivek comes into contact with that need so much help.

That sounds great Sarsha bubbled, so can Nivek take care of the other gems too, for the babies. If that is what you really want with all your heart Manuel responded. Nivek moved closer to Sarshas side, I would be honoured to do so Sarsha. Especially now that I know some of what you have been through and why you were unable to respond with such help before. He gave her a brief hug and stood up to have another look at the beautiful little girl nestled, asleep in Manuel's arms.

Sarsha softly wept for the relief and joy which now filled her heart. Manuel and Nivek moved just a short distance away to leave Sarsha in peace with her thoughts for a while. Sarsha stood up after a while and her dress fell to the ground as Niveks lion and the lion still resting at the foot of the big tree both roared in such a way that it filled the valley below and the village behind them. Manuel turned around smiling at Nivek. As Nivek turned towards the rock to speak to Sarsha he saw that she was not there but only her beautiful gown was there laying on the rock and a huge blue butterfly with gossamer wings arising up towards the large golden lion head silhouette and the golden eagle. The golden eagle had hovered above Lion Monty and Sarsha from the beginning of that special time in the valley. As the blue butterfly lifted above the heads of everyone on top of the rock it seemed for a few moments to grow so big that it blocked out the sun with its spectacular wing span. Sarsha began to fly higher and higher as the sun shone through the beautiful pieces of artwork of those huge gossamer wings. Nothing else could be seen except for an unusual blue light.

Within moments the golden eagle, the golden lion and the blue butterfly had completely disappeared out of sight.

Manuel, why was it so necessary for Sarsha to pick up the baby and wrap it then hand it to you queried Nivek?

That little girl's mother died giving birth to her, so she was never held by her mother. Sarsha also needed to know that at least one baby was going to live and grow into full adulthood after she had held it. If you noticed the specific way she wrapped the little one in the soft cloth, those actions could only be motivated from a heart of love for little babies and small children, it was a way only a loving mother could do. Now when the little one grows up I can share with her that she has been held by a loving mother as she was wrapped in special care and beauty with a great deal of love. Now she will always have something precious to hold on to when things become a struggle for her later in life

Will she be away for long this time Manuel asked Nivek?

Manuel moved closer to him and put one arm on his shoulder and whispered, my dear young friend that will be the last time you will ever see her she has gone permanently to another place of great beauty, and no she definitely won't be back.

Now let us go back to the village and continue to do those things we know how to for the needs of the people.